Josie looked Blad
"Are you okay?" s

"You shouldn't have rus
leg already. Don't risk injuring the other." Her voice was kind, but her words cut him to the quick. "I was worried about you."

He suppressed his irritation, reading between the lines. *You're not strong enough to handle this.*

"I'm absolutely fine," he replied. "But this situation is a lot worse than I imagined. I think I should stay here for a while to help protect you."

Archie lifted his head from his mother's shoulder and smiled. "See, Mom, I told you he was a superhero."

"I already told you, Archie," Josie said gently. "He's only a man."

But Josie was wrong. He wasn't only a man. He was a father, and a fiercely protective streak had torn itself through his body. He sensed her difficulty in forgiving him for vanishing from her life all those years ago, but whatever differences they might have, they would need to work together to ensure that their son's safety came first.

Elisabeth Rees was raised in the Welsh town of Hay-on-Wye, where her father was the parish vicar. She attended Cardiff University and gained a degree in politics. After meeting her husband, they moved to the wild, rolling hills of Carmarthenshire, and Elisabeth took up writing. She is now a full-time wife, mother and author. Find out more about Elisabeth at elisabethrees.com.

Books by Elisabeth Rees

Love Inspired Suspense

Navy SEAL Defenders

Lethal Exposure
Foul Play
Covert Cargo
Unraveling the Past
The SEAL's Secret Child

Caught in the Crosshairs

THE SEAL'S SECRET CHILD

ELISABETH REES

HARLEQUIN® LOVE INSPIRED® SUSPENSE

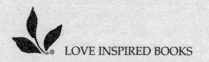

LOVE INSPIRED BOOKS

ISBN-13: 978-0-373-67812-9

The SEAL's Secret Child

Copyright © 2017 by Elisabeth Rees

www.Harlequin.com

Printed in U.S.A.

Come to Me, all you who are weary and burdened,
and I will give you rest. Take My yoke upon you
and learn from Me, for I am gentle and humble in heart,
and you will find rest for your souls.

—Matthew 11:28-29

For Josie, Archie and Morgan.

ONE

Josie Bishop took a deep breath, knelt to the carpet in her son's bedroom and groped around underneath his bed. She was searching for discarded socks and underwear, but instead she found an old orange peel, sticky candy, half-eaten sandwiches and all manner of other unpleasant items that lurk in the depths of a six-year-old boy's bedroom.

Her fingers came to rest on something soft, squishy and furry. She yanked her hand out.

"Archie!" she yelled out. "What are you keeping under your bed?"

The noise woke up Sherbet, Archie's blue parakeet, sitting on a perch in his cage next to the bed.

"Pretty boy. Pretty boy," the budgie squawked, making a bowing motion with his head.

Josie jumped. Sherbet always had a habit of scaring her when she was off guard.

"Be quiet, Sherbet," she muttered, steeling

herself to retrieve the furry object beneath the bed. Pulling out her hand slowly, she found herself staring at a moldy peach, collapsed like a popped balloon. It seemed to sum up how Josie felt: deflated, empty and way past her sell-by date.

The bird chirruped.

"What do you want, Sherbet?" she asked, looking for some scrap paper on which to place the soggy fruit.

The budgie picked up his empty food bowl in his beak and banged it against the bars.

"You want food?" Josie asked, gingerly holding the peach in one hand and reaching for the birdseed with another. "I'm sorry I'm grumpy, but I'm jittery." She poked some seeds through the bars. "And I must also be crazy, because I'm talking to a bird."

Josie nervously peered through the window to see a uniformed officer standing guard outside her home in Sedgwick, Kansas. He had been there for the past five days, ever since a series of threatening phone calls culminated in someone trying to run her off the road on her way home from work. It had been a terrifying experience.

As an attorney working for the Sedgwick County Public Defender Office, Josie had been assigned a child abduction case. It was her job to defend the man accused of abducting a young girl from the sidewalk outside her home. The accused man, Norman Francis, was an odd and reclusive character who always wore a large overcoat even on the sunniest days. Norman claimed that the three-year-old girl came into his neighboring home uninvited, and he proclaimed his innocence. But his protestations were to no avail, and he was subsequently charged with kidnapping. Yet Josie believed his pleas of innocence and had gladly agreed to represent him in court. The community of Sedgwick had already acted as judge and jury, condemning Norman without a trial, and Josie intended to let the truth be told.

However, someone in the vicinity was determined to make her pay for defending a man like Norman, a man who some believed was a potential child abuser. After it became apparent that her life was in danger, the police agreed to post an officer outside on the driveway for a few hours a day to act as a deterrent. Whoever wanted to terrorize her was not going to win.

Despite the fear that had been instilled in Josie, she wouldn't let it destroy her life. After narrowly escaping her attacker's car, she had sat down around the kitchen table with Archie and her father, Tim, to discuss how they would cope. Her dad had lived with her ever since the death of her mother five years ago, and he had been a constant source of support. Being a single mom was hard, and Josie often worked long hours. Her dad stepped in frequently, doing the school runs, making dinner, being a surrogate dad for Archie. She had no idea where her son's real father was. He had vanished many years ago, apparently determined never to be found, despite an extensive search.

Spying a crumpled piece of paper on the windowsill, Josie picked it up and placed it on Archie's desk, intending to wrap the dripping peach and throw it in the trash. It was a sheet from the printer in her son's room. He was a budding engineer and often used a kids' software package to print his crazy designs. But this paper was a printed email conversation, covered in doodles of birds and mice. She furrowed her brow, unaware that Archie had set up his own email address. He knew that this sort of online activity wasn't allowed. As she looked closer, she jumped with shock. The name of the person her son had been conversing with caused her to gasp and drop the fruit to the floor. The peach exploded on the carpet, showering her ankles with a spray of juice, but she didn't care. She simply looked at the paper, too stunned to move.

"Archie," she yelled. "Come here, please."

She held the printed paper with shaking hands, confronted with the name Edward Harding. Josie blinked hard. Edward Harding was the name of her ex-fiancé. Edward Harding was the name of her son's father, a man who had never known of Archie's existence. Could Archie have possibly found his father? Could a six-year-old have managed to complete a job that several private detectives had failed to do?

Archie appeared in the doorway, his blond, unruly curls and freckled face making him appear impish and mischievous. When he saw the paper in his mother's hand, his cheeks flushed, and he looked at the floor guiltily.

"I'm not mad," Josie said gently, leading her son to sit on the bed. "But will you explain this to me?"

She cast her eyes over the email, trying to make out the words behind the doodles. She saw, *mom*, *danger*, *bad man*, *help us*. Archie was asking for assistance from a man who might very well be a complete stranger.

"I saw him on a news channel," Archie said in a small voice. "And I called the news station. They gave me his email address."

"Who did you see, sweetie?" Josie asked. "A man you thought was your dad?"

"It *was* my dad," he replied, imploring her to believe him. "Some bad guys were arrested in Missouri last week, and my dad helped catch them." He pointed to the television in the corner of his room. "A reporter asked him all about it and put it on TV. The man's name was Edward Harding. That's my dad's name, right?"

"Oh, honey," Josie said, sitting on the bed next to her boy and placing an arm around his slim shoulders. "There are probably lots of men named Edward Harding. I know you want to meet your dad, and I've tried really hard to find him, but we have to accept that he's gone."

Archie looked up into her face, his bright blue eyes glittering with the hope of a child. "But this guy had one leg, Mom."

She drew a sharp breath. Archie's father was a former navy SEAL who had lost his lower leg after being injured on a mission in Afghanistan seven years previously. Archie knew this. She had told him as much about his father as he had wanted to know. Which was a lot.

"I know it was him, Mom," Archie continued. "He looked like me." He pointed to a spot on his ear where the cartilage was flattened and smooth. "He even has the same ears."

Josie found her head reeling. "Why didn't you come and talk to me about it?" she asked, attempting to control the unease in her voice. "You should have told me."

Archie looked down at his hands cupped in his lap. "I don't know if you like my dad now," he said quietly. "You never talk about him anymore. I thought you would keep me from seeing him."

"Archie," she said, wrapping her arms around his torso. "Of course I want you to see your dad. I've tried to find him. I really have." She pulled back and wiped tears from beneath her eyes. "It's complicated. It's hard for you to understand. You should never get in touch with a stranger unless you ask me first, okay?"

Archie jumped off the bed and stood with his fists clenched. "But he's not a stranger, Mom. He's my dad." Archie pointed to the email still clutched between Josie's fingers. "He wrote back to me and he was nice. He says he remembers you. I told him you were scared because of the bad man, and he says he can come help us." He pulled himself up to his full height, like a proud soldier. "I know he was in a special army. He can make you safe."

Josie listened to her son with a mixture of terror, bewilderment and disbelief. Was this Edward Harding truly the man she had loved and lost? Could this be the man who had vanished from her life overnight because he couldn't accept his disability? Or was someone cruelly playing a trick on her beautiful little boy, exploiting his desperate desire to meet his father?

"Sweetheart," she said, kneeling to the floor

and clasping Archie by the shoulders. "When did you get in touch with this man?"

"Yesterday."

"And did you tell him where we live?"

Archie nodded solemnly. "He's coming to see us."

Josie's heart skipped. "When?"

When Archie refused to speak, Josie pushed a little harder. "This is really important, Archie," she said. "I need to know when he's coming here to Sedgwick."

But before her son could answer, a loud crash sounded through the room. A brick came through the window and hit the wall, smashing a mirror and then bouncing onto the carpet. Around the brick was a white piece of paper secured with a rubber band. Josie reacted instantly, yanking Archie to the ground, away from the glass, before covering his small body with her own. She could see bold black words written on the paper: DROP THE CASE OR PAY THE PRICE. In the next moment, the police officer who had been stationed out front came bounding into the room.

"Go to the back of the house," he ordered. "And stay away from the windows. Let me deal with this."

Josie scrambled to her feet and lifted her son into her arms. He curled his legs around her waist and she carried him into the kitchen, almost colliding with her dad, Tim, in the hallway.

"What's going on?" Tim asked, his eyes wide and fearful. "What happened?"

"Somebody threw a brick through Archie's window," she replied, holding her hand over her son's head, not wanting to imagine how close he came to serious injury. The person who wanted to terrorize her had no intention of stopping. "Oh, Dad, why does this have to happen to us?"

Her father steered her into the kitchen and pulled down the blinds, shielding them from view to anybody outside.

"The police will do their job, Josie. Don't worry." Yet her father was utterly failing to hide the anxiety in his voice. "It's just somebody trying to scare you. That's all."

Josie hugged Archie even tighter. She felt his breath quicken on her neck.

"It's okay, Granddad," Archie said, keeping a tight hold on his mother. "My dad is coming to help us today. He promised."

Tim's eyebrows shot up high, and he looked sharply at Josie. "What did he just say?"

Josie squeezed her eyes tightly shut. If what her son said was true, then she would shortly be seeing a man who had vanished from her life seven years ago, someone who had no idea she was ever pregnant with his child. After losing his leg, Edward had broken off their engagement via letter and disappeared, severing contact with his friends and family. She had understood why he had done it, but she had never forgiven him. After searching fruitlessly to find him and inform him of the birth of his son, she had eventually given up.

Her stomach was a swirl of dread. How on earth was she going to face the difficult task of allowing him into her life again? She had turned her back on the past and forged a future without him.

"Dad," she said shakily, "you'd better sit down. I have something to tell you."

Blade Harding entered the small town of Sedgwick with a knot the size and weight of a sledgehammer somewhere in his gut. He had been on the road for the last twenty-four hours, driving from his home in North Carolina, only stopping to nap in the truck before setting off again. As each mile clocked on the dash, his heartbeat turned up a notch.

Since losing the lower portion of his left leg to a shrapnel wound seven years ago, Blade had battled a range of destructive and negative feelings before finally reaching acceptance. Now he was fully integrated back into society, running a successful business and enjoying life again.

He was also training for the Invictus Games, where he would compete against other wounded, injured or disabled veterans. He was proud of himself once more, something he never thought would happen. He had even embraced his new life by introducing himself to new people as Blade instead of Edward. It was a nickname that his buddies had given him due to the prosthetic blade he used for running, and it had stuck.

He glanced at the GPS screen on his dash, checking that he was correctly headed for the Kansas address his son had given him. Knowing he was close by triggered an emotion so intense that he had to pull to the side of the road and compose himself. Could he really have a son? When he had first read the childlike email purporting to be from a six-year-old boy, he had dismissed it as the prank of somebody who worked in the auto body shop he owned. The first line of the email was too unbelievable to be true: My name is Archie and I think yoo ar my dad. But after reading more of the poorly spelled words, he found himself astonished and stunned to learn that the boy's mother was Josie Bishop. Only a very small, select group of people knew about Josie. And none of those people would prank him like that.

He had gone over and over events in his mind. Had Josie been pregnant when he'd left for Afghanistan? It was possible. He hadn't been a Christian at the time, and neither was she. They hadn't fully considered the consequences of their actions. But why wouldn't she have told him?

He started out on the road again. He was now just one block away. The knot in his belly tightened. Archie had told him that Josie was in danger and needed help. Somebody was threatening to hurt her. Would she accept help from him? Would she see him? Was the child even his? The questions flying through his head were relentless. But the one thing he most hoped was waiting for him in Kansas was respect and understanding. Since he had become disabled, so many people treated Blade differently, as if he were a weaker man. He was desperate for Josie not to feel this way about him. He wanted her to see him as a complete man.

He pulled into a wide, tree-lined street, instantly spotting a house with a police car outside. The house was single-story, large and well kept, with white shuttered windows and a silver SUV parked in the driveway. His heart lurched to see a police presence and a window boarded up with wood. Given that Archie had already talked of the danger his mother was facing, he knew this must be Josie's home. He rolled the truck to a stop along the curb. But he had no time to steady his nerves, because a police officer walked over to the truck and requested that he roll down the window.

"Can I ask what your business here is?" the officer asked.

"I'm visiting," he replied. "Is everything okay?" He looked at the boarded window. "Has anyone in the house been hurt?"

"We've had some trouble here this evening, but all the occupants are just fine. However, all visitors must be approved by the home owner before exiting their vehicles. Can I take your name, please?"

"It's okay, Officer." A female voice cut through the air, loud and clear with the soft lilt of a Kansas native. He knew instantly that it was Josie. "I've been expecting him."

The officer tipped his hat and stepped aside, allowing Blade to catch sight of Josie for the first time in seven years. She had barely changed, and his breath caught in his throat. Her hair was as red as he remembered, cascading over her shoulders in waves of lava. The intense color was the perfect frame for her china-white skin and striking green eyes. She stood with her arms crossed, wearing a black pencil skirt and a white tailored blouse, looking every inch the beautiful, professional woman. And he was struck temporarily dumb.

"Hello, Edward," she called. "Are you going to come inside?"

He swallowed hard. He was a wreck. He slipped out of the driver's seat and began walking up the path, all the while feeling her gaze on him. She was impossible to read.

"Everybody calls me Blade these days," he said when he reached her. "Edward is who I used to be."

"Well, whatever you call yourself now, we have a lot to discuss," she said flatly as he reached the door. Her defensive posture clearly let him know that any physical contact would be unwelcome.

He looked at the police officer standing on the front lawn. "I didn't realize your situation was so serious," he said. "What happened?"

She ushered him inside and closed the door. "That's not important right now. What's important is introducing you to your son."

Blade put a hand over his belly, which had exploded with butterflies. "So it's true? The child is mine?"

Josie's arms remained crossed. "His name is Archie," she said. "And, yes, he's yours. He's with my dad in the kitchen. I wanted to explain things to you before you met him."

Blade walked into the living room, feeling the need to sit in one of the large wicker chairs.

He rubbed two hands over his face, now stubbly since he hadn't been able to shave for the past twenty-four hours.

"Why didn't you tell me?" he asked, looking at her imploringly. "Seven years have passed, and I had no idea my son was walking this earth without his father."

She let her hands drop to her sides, and he noticed that she was digging her nails into her palms. "When you came back from your mission in Afghanistan, I was already ten weeks pregnant, but I didn't want to tell you the news while you were undergoing intensive medical treatment to try to save your leg." Her eyes flitted to his left pants leg, under which was a carbon fiber prosthetic limb encased in flesh-colored plastic. "So I waited."

Blade stood up. "I had a right to know. You should have told me immediately."

"That's not fair!" she shouted before dropping her voice again. "I had no idea you were about to run out on me. After you had the leg amputated, I thought you'd recover, we'd get married and our family would be complete. But you had other ideas, didn't you?" Her eyes were blazing now. "You just vanished and nobody knew where you were, not even your friends. I had no choice but to move back home to Sedgwick and raise Archie with the help of my parents."

Blade sat heavily in the chair. Her criticism of him was justified. He had behaved in a cowardly way, but he had a good reason for leaving like he did. Or so he'd thought at the time.

"I'm sorry," he said quietly. "When I lost my leg, I was devastated." He looked up at her. "I assumed I couldn't be a good, strong husband for you. I knew I'd be medically discharged from the SEALs, and I had no idea how I'd earn a living. I didn't want to rely on VA disability compensation to provide for my family. I felt useless, and I thought you'd be better off without me, so I decided to disappear."

She sat on the chair opposite him. "You left me a note," she said in a whisper. "That's all. If you'd broken off our engagement in person, I could have explained I was pregnant, but you didn't give me the chance."

"I'm sorry." It was all he could say, but it was hopelessly inadequate. "I thought it was for the best at the time."

She regarded him with steely eyes. "You broke off contact with everybody in your life. Why did you do that?"

Blade hated thinking about this part of his life. It was a dark time. He had no strong family connections, so cutting himself off from distant relatives was easy, but abandoning Josie and his friends shamed him.

"I was grieving," he said. "I didn't want to be reminded of my old life, when I was strong and able-bodied. I just shut down." He held his hands up. "I know it was selfish, but it was the only thing I could do."

Josie put her head in her hands, letting her hair envelop her fingers. "I tried to stay in touch with your old SEAL buddies so that I would know when you resurfaced, but over the years, I lost contact."

"I'm guessing you never told any of them you were pregnant," he said. "Otherwise they would've let me know."

Josie twined her fingers together. "I didn't want you to hear the news from a third party. I assumed I'd find a way to contact you, but before I knew it, I was all out of leads." She raised her head and locked eyes with him. "I would never intentionally keep your son from you. I prayed so hard for an answer."

He smiled weakly at her. It looked like she shared his Christian faith now. It was comforting. "After I left Virginia, I went down to Florida and lived there for four years, working for a motor mechanic business. I was just bumming around with no direction and no hope. I wanted to drop off the radar. But then I met an athlete who competes in the Invictus Games, and he turned my life around. I started training with him, and I learned to be proud of myself again. I got back in touch with my SEAL buddies through the military support unit, and I moved back to my hometown in North Carolina." He felt himself welling up. "But this is all irrelevant now." He looked at the doorway that he assumed led into the kitchen. "What I really want to do is meet my son."

Josie stood up, wiping her moist palms on her skirt. "Archie says he saw you on the news and contacted you through the station. Is that right?"

"That's right," Blade replied. "Do you remember my old buddy Tyler?"

She nodded.

"I helped him catch the leader of a meth gang in Missouri recently. He's a sheriff there. It's a long story, but a national news station came to interview me about it. When I got back to North Carolina, there was an email waiting for me from Archie. He'd recognized my name and gotten my email address from the news station." He smiled. "He's a smart kid."

"Yes, he is," Josie said. "But why didn't you contact me when he sent you the email? Surely that would have been the best option. And then I could've been better prepared for this moment."

"I tried," Blade replied. "But your number isn't listed, and Archie wouldn't tell me what it was. He thought you might try to stop me from coming. He said you were in trouble and needed somebody to protect you. I just had to get here right away, so I hopped in my truck and drove through the night." Every moment that passed was another moment without his son. "Please, Josie, can I meet Archie now? I'm dying here."

"Of course," she said, extending her hand toward him. "Can I help you out of the chair?"

He briefly hung his head and sighed. So his most important question had now been answered. Josie *did* see him as a weaker man. And he was bitterly disappointed.

"No, thanks," he said, standing with ease. "I'm good."

She walked briskly to the doorway and closed her fingers around the handle. "Are you ready?"

Blade's heart began to hammer. Would he ever be ready for this moment? "Absolutely."

With that, Josie opened the door. "Archie, your dad is here to see you."

Josie's emotions ran rampant as she watched Blade kneel to the floor and hug his son for the first time. She saw a tear fall down Blade's stubbly face, and she fought hard to suppress tears of her own. The instant love that her ex-fiancé felt for his son was clear to see, and his embrace was fierce yet gentle. It made her think of a father bear cradling a cub. But at the same time,

Blade's presence here caused her chest to ache with regret and pain. Could she ever forgive this man for abandoning her when she needed him most?

Archie, meanwhile, took this profound moment in stride.

"Hi, Dad," he said, as if it were an everyday occurrence to hug his father. "I knew you would come."

Blade pulled back. "Thank you for finding me, Archie."

Archie smiled broadly, his freckled face a picture of innocence. "Which one of your legs was chopped off?" He glanced between the right and left. "They both look the same."

Blade laughed heartily, throwing back his head the way he always used to. His mop of curly hair was as unruly as ever, just like his son's, and his rugged face had gotten even more handsome over the years. His strong and chiseled jawline was hidden by beard growth, but his Roman nose was still his most prominent feature, the high bridge settled between his piercing blue eyes.

"I'll show you if you like," Blade replied, pulling up the left leg of his jeans. He knocked on the pink plastic beneath, making a hard clunking sound.

"Wow!" Archie said with genuine admiration. "Just like a superhero."

Blade winked. "I keep my cape in the truck."

Josie saw her father hanging back nervously. She coughed. "Edward...I mean, Blade, you remember my dad, right?"

"Sure I do," Blade replied, holding his hand out to shake Tim's. "It's good to see you again, Tim." He glanced around. "So where's Martha?"

Tim looked at his feet.

"Mom died five years ago," Josie said, saving her father the difficulty of answering. "Cancer."

A look of pain swept over Blade's face. "Oh, I'm so sorry."

"You have a lot of catching up to do," Josie said. "An awful lot."

"So," Blade said, pulling a chair from the table and sitting on it. "Let's start from the beginning." He put two strong hands in his son's armpits and pulled the child onto his lap. "I'm all ears."

But as Josie reached for the coffeepot, a series of shots rang out, seeming to come from her front lawn. She screamed and rushed to take Archie from Blade's lap.

"It's the bad man," Archie said, curling his arms around his mother's neck as she lifted him up.

Blade's demeanor changed to one of total control, rushing down the hallway to the front door. "I have a gun in my truck," he said. "Stay here and keep out of sight. I'll be back soon."

"Blade, no," Josie said, watching him peer through the glass panel in the door as the shots ceased. "It's too dangerous for you. Let the police take care of it."

But he didn't answer. He silently slipped through the door and closed it behind him, leaving Josie and her father staring at each other in silence, neither believing that somebody was firing a gun outside their home.

"Dad can save us now," Archie said. "He'll get his cape from his truck."

"He's not really a superhero, honey," Josie said. "He's just a man."

She sat on a chair, waiting for the danger to pass, wondering how she could keep her family safe from this escalating level of threat. She must try to shield Archie. But how? The only thing she could do was close her eyes and pray.

"There's a shooter across the street," the officer called to Blade from his protected position behind his cruiser. "He's reloading. I've radioed for backup. Go inside, sir."

Then the officer began firing at a black sedan parked just a few feet away, giving Blade the perfect cover to run to his truck at the curb.

"My son is in this home," Blade called back, opening the door to his truck and reaching into the glove compartment for his weapon. "There's no way I'm staying inside."

He lifted his head over the hood of the truck to see the barrel of a gun poking through the window of the black car. The officer's firing was opening up a series of holes along the metal, but Blade couldn't see a person inside. The attacker must have been well shielded from the bullets because he seemed unharmed as his gun burst into action again, aimed squarely at Josie's home. Windows shattered, tree bark spit onto the lawn and holes appeared in the yellow front door.

Blade thought of Josie inside, cradling Archie in her arms, and he began to see red. This was the family he never knew he had, and something primal stirred deep within him. He knew he had to protect them at all costs. He had no idea how he would fit into their lives, but he had arrived just in the nick of time. While he suspected that Josie might have doubts about his ability to take care of them, he had none.

Rising from behind the truck, he took aim and fired back. Opposite Josie's home were open fields, and his shots echoed across the grasslands, the noise of each bullet magnified tenfold. Blade managed to hit the car's side mirror, taking it clean off. It obviously spooked the shooter enough to send him scrambling up from his hiding position in the car and into the driver's seat. He raced away from the house, tires squealing on the frosty asphalt on the cold January morning. Blade gave chase, hoping to stop the car in its tracks, but he saw it round a corner and disappear out of sight before he could get an accurate shot.

He ran back to his truck to pursue, only to be confronted with a deflated front tire peppered with bullet holes. He sighed and holstered his weapon, rubbing his forehead in frustration.

The police officer spoke rapidly into his radio, relaying the information to patrol units, giving a description of the vehicle.

Blade walked back up the path to Josie's home. When he opened the door, he saw her standing in the hallway, gripping their son tightly, her father to her side with an arm around her shoulder.

"Did he get away?" she asked.

Blade nodded. "I'm sorry."

Josie's face crumpled, but she composed herself quickly, taking a deep breath and holding on to her father for reassurance.

She looked Blade up and down. "Are you okay? You shouldn't have rushed out like that. You lost one leg already. Don't risk injuring the other." Her voice was kind, but her words cut him to the quick. "I was worried about you."

He suppressed his irritation, reading between the lines: *You're not strong enough to handle this.*

"I'm absolutely fine," he replied. "But this situation is a lot worse than I imagined. I think I should stay here for a while to help protect you."

Archie lifted his head from his mother's shoulder and smiled. "See, Mom, I told you he was a superhero."

"I already told you, Archie," Josie said gently. "He's only a man."

Blade knew it would be a challenge to insert himself into their lives under these circumstances. Josie would need time to accept his presence, and the existence of danger would make it doubly hard.

But Josie was wrong. He wasn't only a man. He was a father, and a fiercely protective streak had torn itself through his body. He sensed her difficulty in forgiving him for vanishing from her life all those years ago, but whatever differences they might have, they would need to work together to ensure that their son's safety came first. It would require all of his patience to work closely with Josie. Her throwaway comments had already confirmed his worst fears: she didn't see him as an equal to an able-bodied man. He had briefly wondered whether their reunion would reignite a spark, but he was wrong. He could never get close to a woman who treated him with pity or who tried to shield him from danger because of his disability. No way.

He was a complete man. And he intended to prove it. This time, he would go the distance.

TWO

Josie sat in her kitchen, opposite Blade, jiggling her foot anxiously. She kept stealing glances at her old flame, still struggling to come to terms with the fact that he was actually there in her home. Even though she had wished him back in her life for the sake of her son, now that this scenario had become reality, it was a bitter pill to swallow.

She was getting along just fine as a single mom, and was used to being the sole decision-maker in matters relating to Archie's well-being. Now all of a sudden, her son's father had a right to demand an equal say. The shooting incident had terrified her and she wanted to get Archie as far away from Sedgwick as possible until the danger had been neutralized. But would she and Blade disagree on the best way forward?

Two detectives from Wichita were also seated in her kitchen. They had been summoned by the public defender's office to oversee protection for Josie and her family. Detectives Dave Pullman and Carly Sykes had completed a thorough crime scene examination and interviewed Blade, Tim and Archie before asking to discuss a plan of action with Josie. Meanwhile, uniformed officers began to sweep the glass and board up the broken windows. Blade insisted on remaining with Josie while Tim and Archie packed some bags in preparation for leaving. Staying in their home now was impossible.

"You two are Archie's parents, right?" Detective Sykes began. "This must be a pretty scary time for you folks, but your son seems to be taking it all in stride." She smiled at Blade. "He places a lot of faith in his father to come to the rescue. He's a really sweet kid."

Blade smiled. "Yes, he is. I'm proud of him."

Josie bristled. Blade had only just met Archie, yet he was taking the credit for how he'd turned out. It wasn't fair.

"Can we get to the point?" she asked. "I'd like to make plans as quickly as possible."

"Sure," Detective Sykes replied briskly. "I understand that a brick was thrown through your window this morning. And there was a note wrapped around that brick."

Blade looked sharply at Josie, his face full of concern.

"Yes," she said. "The police officer stationed

outside my home said it was thrown from the same vehicle that returned later with a shooter inside. It matches the description of a car that tried to run me off the road a couple of weeks back."

The detective checked an entry in her notepad. "Unfortunately, this car was stolen from Wichita last month, so it doesn't lead us to the perp, but we've put out a description to all our patrols."

Blade leaned toward Josie. "What did it say?" he whispered.

She was confused. "What did what say?"

"The note around the brick."

"Oh, that." She closed her eyes, not caring to remember the hastily scrawled capital letters. "It said, 'Drop the case or pay the price.'"

"We've been told that you've also been receiving abusive phone calls and letters," Detective Pullman said. "They're all related to a current case you're working on at the public defender's office, right?"

Josie nodded.

"I think it's awesome that you're a public defender," Blade said admiringly. "No matter what's happening right now, you should be proud of yourself."

She ignored the praise. "I worked hard to establish myself as a good attorney," she said, silently adding in her head, *while you were busy finding yourself in Florida.* "It was difficult, but my parents helped out a lot with babysitting Archie."

"I need to know the background to this case," Blade said. "Can you explain the details to me?"

"I don't think there's any point. The police have got it under control."

He furrowed his brow. "It doesn't look that way to me. Please, Josie, just give me a little more information. I might be able to help. Don't forget about my background."

How could she forget his history in the military? It was the SEALs who cost him his leg. It was the SEALs who destroyed their relationship.

"That was a long time ago," she said. "You're a different man now."

She saw a look of irritation fall across his face. "I'm not so different that I can't step up and help protect you. It won't hurt to give me a little background information, will it?"

Detective Sykes seemed to sense the atmosphere grow a little cooler and gave a light cough as if to cover her embarrassment.

"It would be useful if you went over the details with us as well," she said. "We've only just been assigned this case, and although we have the incident reports to read, it would help us to hear the full story in your own words."

"Okay," she said, taking a deep breath to run

through the events yet again. "I'm currently defending a client named Norman Francis, who's been accused of kidnapping a three-year-old girl, Lisa Brown, from outside her home almost two years ago. Lisa and her parents lived across the street from him. A neighbor of Norman's telephoned the police one evening and claimed that she saw Norman drag the little girl from the sidewalk and into his home. The police responded immediately, entered Norman's house and found Lisa in the kitchen, unharmed and helping herself to cookies from a jar. Norman said he had been in his living room for the previous two hours, carving figurines that he sells at craft fairs. He claimed to have no idea that the girl was in his kitchen and asserted that she must have walked in through his unlocked back door of her own accord. But the witness testimony from the neighbor helped to build a strong case against him, and he was subsequently arrested and charged with child abduction. But I believe his story. I don't think he did it."

"What did the child say?" Detective Pullman asked.

"Lisa was interviewed by specially trained officers, but due to her age, it was very difficult to get a consistent account of what happened. She started off saying that she went into the house by herself but subsequently changed her story to claim that Norman led her inside with a promise of candy. Then, a little later, she said that Cinderella took her inside." Josie rubbed her index fingers on her temples. "She's simply not a credible witness, so the prosecution decided not to include her testimony. But she was examined and found to have no injuries, so there's no forensic evidence to label Norman as an abuser." She shrugged. "That doesn't stop people from gossiping, though."

"I guess a small place like Sedgwick is full of rumors and amateur detectives," Blade said. "So this Norman guy has already been judged guilty."

"Correct," confirmed Josie. "He's kinda odd. Before all this happened, he hardly ever went out, but when he did, he always wore a huge padded coat and kept his head bent low like he didn't want to be noticed. It was only after I agreed to represent him that I found out he suffers from cerebral palsy, which limits the movement of his right arm and leg. He wears the big coat to hide his arm, and he walks in a shuffling sort of way to compensate for his leg. He was bullied a lot as a youngster, so he's a very secretive person and doesn't want people to notice his disability."

Josie glanced at Blade. He appeared to be listening carefully to her every word. Maybe Norman's experience resonated with him. Perhaps he also suffered the same negative response from society because of his missing limb. Thankfully, she was sensitive to the needs of those with disabilities and always made sure she phrased her words carefully to avoid giving offense. But others were not so tactful.

"It takes a really long time to prepare for a trial," she continued. "So for the last eighteen months, I've been building Norman's defense case and overseeing all the trial preliminaries. I know a lot of people in Sedgwick think that Norman's guilty, and I sometimes get yelled at on the street, but things really started to escalate about three weeks ago. That's when I received the first anonymous letter. Then the phone calls started. It's always a muffled man's voice saying I'll suffer for defending a monster like Norman. I used to ask who he was, but now I just hang up."

"And how is Norman doing?" Detective Pullman asked. "I understand that he's out on bail."

"Norman's required to wear an electronic tag as part of his bail conditions," Josie replied. "So he's housebound. He used his home as collateral to raise the bond, and I had to fight hard to get bail granted. Norman has precise physical needs, and his home is specially adapted to suit him, so the judge agreed to bail Norman on the condition that he never leaves his home. Norman was so distressed about news of his disability leaking out to the community that the judge allowed the hearing to be a closed one, and the media didn't get to hear the details. It's unusual for a judge to agree to something like this, but I successfully argued that revealing Norman's medical history to an open court would have caused him psychological damage. Of course, now everybody assumes he has something sinister to hide."

"What about the little girl?" Detective Sykes asked. "Surely her family doesn't want to be living in proximity to their child's alleged kidnapper."

"The Brown family moved from the street within a few weeks of the incident, so there's no chance of Norman running into them." She shrugged. "But Norman never goes outside, anyway. He's too terrified. The community doesn't want him back in their neighborhood, and he knows it."

"But how does he manage being housebound?" Blade asked. "He has to eat."

"I take groceries to him once a week and make sure he's okay."

Detective Pullman raised an eyebrow. "It sounds like you're dedicating a lot of your schedule to this client. How do you find the time to work on anything else?"

"Norman is my only client until the trial is over," Josie said. "Since I became the target of threats, the public defender's office decided to allocate my other cases to alternate attorneys. I simply can't offer anybody else quality service while this situation continues, so Norman gets me all to himself. And it's probably a good thing, as he has nobody else to take care of him right now."

"But he's not in danger, is he?" Blade asked. "He's not getting bricks through his window or nasty phone calls?"

"No," she replied. "That's the odd thing. The letters and phone calls have been directed at me." She stopped to steady her voice. "And now it's gone way beyond that. Now somebody doesn't just want to frighten me. They want to kill me."

Detective Sykes closed her notepad. "This situation does appear to have intensified in these last few hours, and it's now too serious for the Sedgwick Police Department to monitor. I recommend that you and your family move to a safe house for the duration of the trial. The public defender's office has informed us that they will spare no expense in ensuring your protection."

"Neither will I," Blade said. He turned to Josie. "I'll make some calls and put a temporary manager in charge of my business so I can stay here in Sedgwick for however long it takes."

Josie found her mouth dropping in disbelief. "*You* want to come to a safe house with us."

"Of course," he replied as if the question was ridiculous. "I promised Archie that I'd take care of you, and I meant it."

She began to panic, imagining being forced to spend each day with the man she had once loved but no longer knew. "But…but…my dad and I are perfectly capable of looking after my son by ourselves."

"*Our* son," Blade corrected her. "Archie is mine, too."

"I know," she said. "But I've been taking care of him by myself for such a long time. It would be difficult for him to adjust to his father's sudden presence in his life every day." She knew this was a lame excuse, designed to suit her delicate emotions rather than Archie's. "We should wait until this is all over before making visitation arrangements."

Blade's expression looked genuinely hurt and, for a few moments, Josie deeply regretted her words. After all, she had dreamed of the day when her son would finally meet his father, fulfilling his longest-held wish. This should have been a day of joy for her. So why did she feel so tormented inside? Why did she feel that Archie might be slipping from her grasp?

"I don't want to wait," Blade said quietly. "I want to be around constantly to make sure that you're both okay."

The detectives clearly sensed the need to give the two parents time alone to discuss the matter, and they both rose in unison.

"We'll give you a few minutes to talk it over," Detective Pullman said. "We'll go check on the progress of the cleanup."

"Thank you," Josie said. "I'll be ready to leave soon, I promise."

As soon as the detectives had left the room, Blade went to sit close to Josie.

"Why do I get the feeling you'd rather I wasn't here?" he asked. "Are you sorry that Archie found me?"

"No, not at all."

Blade's blue eyes were wide and intense, a mirror image of Archie's. "So why the reluctance to let me stay with you?"

"Because..." She struggled to find any words that wouldn't make her sound like the most selfish, awful person in the world. "Because I never felt such primal and fierce love before Archie came along. I would literally kill anybody who tried to hurt my son." She shook her head. "*Our* son. And I've been solely responsible for his welfare until now."

Blade obviously knew exactly what she was trying to say. "And you don't think you can share him twenty-four hours a day."

She crossed her arms and sighed. He had hit

the nail on the head. Yes, she most definitely was the most selfish, awful person in the world.

"No, it's not that," she protested weakly, before bowing her head in shame. "Actually, you're right. I always wanted you in his life, but I never knew how hard it would be until this moment."

Blade put a hand on her shoulder. His fingers applied a gentle pressure, and she felt their warmth through her thin cashmere cardigan.

"We're only just learning how to do this," he said. "Let's take it one step at a time. I'll try to be sensitive to your feelings and not tread on your toes, but I have a right to be with our son while he faces such a serious threat."

Josie nodded. "Of course you do." She silently admonished herself. "You're very welcome to come with us to the safe house."

"Thank you."

She rose from the chair. "I'll need to go pack some things."

In truth, she was desperate to get away from Blade, to gather her thoughts and say a prayer to soothe all her anxieties and fears.

"Sure," he said, standing with her.

She brushed past him and headed out the door, not knowing which aspect of today's developments had scared her the most. Was it the man taking aim at her home with a gun, or the man taking aim at her son's heart with a fatherly love that potentially would usurp her own?

Blade watched his son struggle toward the door, clutching a stuffed dog in one hand and a huge birdcage in the other, covered with a white sheet. Josie was a couple of paces behind, also struggling with a suitcase on wheels and a huge file of papers.

He stepped forward and reached for the handle of the case in Josie's hand. "I've got this."

"It's better if I keep it," she said. "It's heavy and awkward."

"All the more reason for me to take it," he said, casting aside her concerned expression with a smile and pulling the case from her grasp. "I'm more than capable." She didn't look convinced, and the smile became fixed on his face. "I'll put it in the car."

He then turned to Archie and knelt to the floor. Just looking at the boy's face still took his breath away. The freckles, the piercing blue eyes, the impish grin and blond curls—they were all features that could be clearly seen in old photographs of him as a child.

"Who is this little guy?" Blade asked, pointing to the black-and-white toy dog.

"It's Oscar," Archie replied. He held up the cage. "And this is Sherbet. He's a blue parakeet and he's two years old. I'm covering him so he doesn't get scared by the lights on the police car."

"It's okay," Blade replied. "It's an unmarked car, and they won't be using any flashing lights." He lifted up the sheet to see a small bird with a beautiful bright blue chest sitting on a perch. The long tapered tail bobbed up and down as the bird edged along the perch, his inquisitive black eyes instantly responding to the human face studying him.

Archie bent his head to peek under the sheet. "Say hello to my dad, Sherbet," he said. "He's looking after us now." The level of pride in his voice was unmistakable.

Blade quickly swallowed the emotion forcing its way to the surface. He'd become a dad overnight and was constantly awestruck.

"Hello, Sherbet," he said, focusing all his attention on the bird so Archie wouldn't see the moisture collecting in his eyes.

"Hello, hello, hello," Sherbet chirruped.

"That was the first word he ever learned," Archie said. "He says it a lot. But he can say tons of other stuff, too. I'll show you when we get to our new house."

"I'd like that," Blade replied, taking the cage from Archie's hand. "Why don't you let me carry this for you? It's kinda big."

Archie gave up the birdcage without a fight

and grabbed hold of Blade's shirt with his free hand. The small gesture of vulnerability was enough to bring the tears back to Blade's eyes. Man, this was killing him, but not in a bad way. The instant love he felt for this small child seemed to produce enough power to knock him right off his feet. Seven years ago, he had assumed he was not a sufficient man to be a good husband and potential father. He had written himself off as worthless. But now was his chance to prove his worth. Now he could be the man he had failed to be back then, even if Josie doubted his physical capabilities.

It was then that he noticed her watching his and Archie's interaction. She was standing by the front door, where the two Wichita detectives were waiting to escort them to the vehicles outside. She was smiling, yet there was sadness in her eyes, and she was biting down on her lip and furrowing her brow.

"You two look like you're getting on well," she said, grinning a little too brightly. "You both have the same nose, you know that?"

"No way!" Archie exclaimed. "Mine is *not* that big."

Blade laughed. "Not yet, son, but just you wait."

Detective Sykes turned the knob on the front door. "Are you ready to leave, Miss Bishop?" she asked. "Your father is already in one of the cars. We'll have to go in two vehicles. Would you like to ride with your dad or your son?"

"My son," she replied quickly. "I'll ride with my son."

Archie let go of his father's shirt and walked to his mother's side. But he turned and looked at Blade earnestly. "Are you okay riding with Granddad?" he asked. "He's really funny and he knows a lot of jokes, but don't let him tell you the one about how to make a tissue dance because it's gross."

Blade smiled. "How so?"

Archie stuck out his tongue and pretended to gag. "Because you put a little boogie into it."

Blade laughed out loud. "It sounds like your granddad has a good sense of humor. I'd love to ride with him."

Detective Sykes opened the door. The January air was damp and chill, seemingly charged with an ominous threat. Was someone waiting for Josie to show herself? Blade automatically positioned himself in front of her and Archie, but he couldn't rest his fingers on his holstered weapon. In one hand, he held the birdcage, and in the other, he wheeled Josie's huge suitcase. He hadn't thought this through.

"Mr. Harding," Detective Sykes said. "You get

into the second vehicle with Detective Pullman. I'll be with Josie and Archie, leading the way."

Blade walked down the path, checking the vicinity all the while. The street was quiet. It was just a few days after New Year's, so everybody was probably taking down decorations and recovering from the overindulgence of the last couple of weeks. Blade didn't like things quiet. He'd spent far too long in his own company, wallowing in self-pity, shutting himself off from the world. It was as though he'd been through a long, dark tunnel, finally emerging into the light with the help of a fellow wounded soldier named Peter.

Peter had handed Blade a Christian leaflet on the street one day, and the words written on it had spoken directly to him: *"Does your life have no meaning?"* Blade had felt that way ever since losing his leg, so he had stopped to chat before accepting an invitation to attend a church meeting, where Peter had surprised and amazed him by revealing his own story. He, too, was a wounded veteran, a double amputee injured in the field in Afghanistan, yet he was an athlete, having competed in the first Invictus Games. Peter had shown Blade that the love and grace of God might not be able to give him a new leg, but they could give him a new purpose. That was his turning point. He became a new man, looking after himself, working out, becoming strong and fit again. And now he was an athlete like Peter, looking forward to competing in his own Invictus Games.

But it looked as though the Lord had a new challenge for him: protecting his newfound family. Even though his relationship with Josie was well and truly over, its legacy meant that he was intrinsically bound to her forever.

Tim opened the trunk to allow Blade to put Josie's case inside. "So you're riding with me, huh?" he said with a kind smile. "It'll give us a chance to talk." He glanced at the birdcage in Blade's hand. "I think you'd better keep Sherbet on your lap."

Blade craned his neck to check that Josie and Archie were safely in the leading vehicle. Then he walked to his truck and pulled out a bag containing some clothes. When he'd left North Carolina, he had no idea how long he might be away, but he'd come prepared. He also picked up the black case containing his carbon fiber, reinforced polymer running blade. He wanted to continue training wherever they might go. Once he'd placed these items into the trunk of the SUV, he slid into the backseat, positioning Sherbet between him and Tim. Detective Pullman was in the driver's seat, engine running.

"All ready?" the detective asked. "It's only a short trip. Thirty minutes or so."

The SUV pulled smoothly into the road, and Blade waited for Tim to start speaking. He had met him only once, shortly after he and Josie had gotten engaged. He guessed that Tim might harbor some resentment toward him for the mistakes of his past.

"It's really good to see you, Blade," Tim said finally. "I always knew you'd show up eventually, and I tried to be a good father figure to Archie until that time. I hope I've done a good job."

Blade was taken aback and more than a little humbled by these words. "You've done a great job, Tim," he said. "I can't thank you enough."

Both men fell into an awkward silence. Neither seemed to know what to say next. Blade spoke first. There was so much he had to say that it came out in one big push.

"I'm sorry that I abandoned your daughter seven years ago, sir. I stupidly thought that she'd be better off without me in her life. If I'd known she was pregnant, I'd never have left. Meeting my son for the first time has blown me away, and I can assure you that I will be ever-present in his life from now on. I love him."

Tim was listening intently, his gray eyes creased at the corners and his balding head tilted slightly in concentration. "What about Josie? Do you love her, too?"

Blade wanted to give the question the careful consideration it deserved, so he took a while to answer. "I did love her. To tell you the truth, she's the only woman I've ever loved. But we've both moved on now. I sense that she's a little hostile toward me, and I totally understand why. She has every right to be angry."

"She's not angry," Tim said. "She's hurt, and she wants you to make it better."

Blade wasn't quite sure what Tim was asking of him. "I can't rewrite the past. I can't make anything better."

Tim shook his head. "I'm not suggesting that you rewrite the past," he said. "I'm suggesting that you write the future. You say that Josie is the only woman you've ever loved. Well, I happen to know that you are the only man she's ever loved, and probably ever *will* love."

Blade couldn't help but laugh. "Josie doesn't love me. Not anymore."

Tim sighed in exasperation. "Maybe not, but she could fall in love with you again."

"I'm sorry, Tim," Blade said, feeling an urgent need to quash these unrealistic hopes. "I know you want this story to have a happy ending, but Josie and I are two totally different people now.

To tell you the truth, I get the feeling she doesn't see me as a strong protector."

Tim seemed surprised. "You do?"

"Since I lost my leg, I've gotten used to people treating me differently, assuming that I'm somehow weak and fragile. I know they're well-intentioned, so I say nothing. But I'd never tolerate that attitude from somebody close to me." He gave a soft laugh. "Maybe that's why I've never fallen in love again. I'm waiting for a woman who treats me like a man with two legs."

Tim mulled over his next words for quite a while before saying, "Doesn't Josie treat you like a man with two legs?"

"No. She doesn't even think I'm capable enough to carry a heavy suitcase, let alone chase down the bad guys." He looked out the window wistfully. "She doesn't see me the way she used to. She patronizes me."

"Don't you think you should talk to her about the way you feel?"

"No," Blade replied quickly. "Our relationship is already pretty rocky. I don't want to make it even more uncomfortable, so I'd appreciate you keeping this conversation between ourselves."

"I think you should be open with her," Tim said. "She probably doesn't realize that her comments are hurtful."

Blade shook his head. "She's likely to be defensive, and I'd rather not start off on the wrong foot." He laughed again. "Although I have only one foot to start off with anyway."

He then noticed Detective Pullman pick up the radio and put it to his mouth. "Carly, I think we're being tailed. I recommend evasive action. Let's go off our designated route."

Blade spun his head around to get a view of the pursuing vehicle. Behind them was the same stolen black sedan that had been parked across the street earlier, showing ragged signs of the earlier gun battle. As soon as Blade's eyes came to rest on the man sitting behind the wheel, the car surged forward, ramming into the SUV's bumper and sending the vehicle lurching forward.

"Carly!" Detective Pullman shouted into the radio. "Let's move. Now!"

Josie put her arm around Archie and pulled him close, placing her hand on his chest. His heartbeat was strong and steady, whereas her heart was beating like a jackhammer. Detective Sykes was driving at top speed, weaving her way through the quiet streets of Sedgwick in an attempt to lose the car pursuing them.

"It's okay, Mom," Archie said, taking her hand. "Dad's in the car behind. He won't let the bad man get to us."

Josie closed her eyes and pulled Archie closer. Her son had built up an aura of invincibility surrounding his father. He knew that his father had been in the navy SEALs and, consequently, believed him to be some kind of all-conquering hero. But Josie knew different. Josie knew that Blade was a man with weaknesses and failings like any other. Yet she couldn't burst her son's bubble by telling him this. And she definitely couldn't compete with the rough-and-tough persona that Archie had allocated to Blade. She felt sidelined.

"Hold tight, guys," Detective Sykes said, taking a sharp left and sending Josie and Archie leaning heavily to the side. "Don't worry. We're taking the scenic route to your new house."

"We're not worried," Josie said, forcing brightness into her voice.

"I hope Sherbet is okay," Archie said, looking up into his mother's face. "I should have brought him with me."

"I'm sure he's fine, honey," Josie said, craning her neck to look back. She saw Detective Pullman at the wheel of the second SUV close behind. She could just make out the outlines of Blade and her dad in the seats behind him. Blade was positioned in a way that allowed him to observe the car on their tail, and she wished that her son was correct in his assumption that his father was invincible. They sure could use a hero right now. But she couldn't expect Blade to be the action man he used to be. It simply wasn't possible anymore.

She saw Detective Pullman look in his rear-view mirror and open his mouth, seeming to shout a warning to his passengers. The SUV pitched forward, having been hit from behind by the pursuer, and the vehicle momentarily mounted the curb, ramming into a fire hydrant so hard that a loud bang sounded. The tire had blown. They were sitting ducks.

"They're in trouble!" Josie shouted. "We should help them."

"We don't stop unless we have to," Detective Sykes said. "We follow protocol."

Then, quick as a flash, Blade jumped from the car and, using the open door as a shield, he began firing rapidly into the windshield of the black sedan, shattering the glass and creating an explosion of noise. Detective Sykes eased off the gas and took their vehicle to the end of the street before stopping at the side of the road and looking around to observe the scene anxiously. She picked up her radio and requested backup, shouting over the noise of firing bullets.

Josie put her hands over her son's ears and held his head on her chest.

"It's okay," she whispered into his ear. "It's all under control."

Looking back, she saw that Blade had been joined by Detective Pullman. Both men fired on the black sedan, alternately shouting orders for the man to exit the vehicle with his hands up. But this guy had taken cover by crouching beneath the dash and clearly had no intention of showing himself. Instead he put the car in Reverse, floored the gas pedal and careened backward, the tires squealing and smoking on the asphalt. He mounted the curb, veering wildly from side to side, but managed to bring the vehicle back onto the road and perform a skidding turn. Then he raced away, vanishing from sight in just a few seconds.

Josie took her hands away from Archie's ears and smiled at him. "The bad man has gone."

Blade appeared at the passenger side of their SUV, alert and watchful. He opened the door. "Tim and I will ride with you while Detective Pullman stays with his damaged vehicle," he said, reaching into the backseat and touching his son's cheek. "You okay, kiddo? That was a bit scary, huh?"

Josie could see that a look of apprehension had crept onto Archie's face. "Where's Granddad? And where's Sherbet?" He looked around. "He didn't fly away, did he?"

"Granddad's right here," Blade said, opening the back door to allow Tim inside. "And he's got Sherbet with him, so scooch over and make some room."

Josie could hear the smooth, even tone of Blade's voice, yet he couldn't mask his urgency to leave this situation behind.

Detective Sykes turned to Josie. "Detective Pullman will be just fine here until backup arrives, and he'll ensure that the black sedan doesn't come our way."

"There's no way that his vehicle will get very far," Blade said, sliding into the passenger seat and securing his belt. "The engine was pouring smoke from bullet damage. I figure he'll be caught soon enough."

Josie looked down at her hands. She knew that these were hollow words, designed to comfort and reassure. This criminal was determined to catch her, determined to make her pay a heavy price for representing Norman Francis. And she had no doubt in her mind that he was already long gone, plotting how to find her and when to launch his next attack.

She watched Archie lift the blanket on the birdcage and talk to Sherbet in a gentle voice. Her son was the most tender and kindhearted child in the world. He didn't deserve this level of threat in his life. It just wasn't fair. While *she* could take the danger and the risk, Archie was just a six-year-old boy. He was innocent of any wrongdoing.

There was nothing else to do. She would have to send him away until the danger had passed, whether Blade liked it or not.

THREE

Josie had barely spoken a word to Blade since arriving at the safe house. She was distracted, preoccupied and jittery, hardly surprising under the circumstances, but he sensed that something else was weighing heavily on her mind—something more than the narrow escape from her attacker. She was pacing the hallway, stressing about her missing suitcase.

"Relax," Blade said. "Detective Pullman will be here soon. Why don't you sit in the living room with Detective Sykes while I make some iced tea?"

As she shook her head, Archie's voice echoed through the house. "Mom, Mom," he called, tearing down the stairs. "You should see my room. It's got a jungle painted on the wall." He took a deep breath and splayed his fingers in the air, pausing for dramatic effect. "Including tons of parrots. Sherbet loves it. It's like being back in the wild." He turned to Blade, his expression changing to an earnest one. "Budgies don't actually live in the jungle. They are knave to Australia, but Sherbet doesn't know that."

"The word is *native*, honey," Josie said. "Budgies are native to Australia."

Blade smiled at his son. "You are such a smart kid, you know that? I had no idea that parakeets come from Australia."

"I know all about parakeets," Archie said, already climbing the stairs to return to his cool new room. "I can teach you." He continued speaking even as he rounded the bend in the stairs and disappeared from view. "Boy budgies talk better than girl budgies. That's why I got a boy."

Josie pulled her cashmere cardigan tightly around her waist as she stared up the empty staircase. "He sure loves that budgie," she said in a faraway tone. "It's his best friend."

"Are you okay?" Blade asked, going to stand next to her in the wide hallway. "Do you like the house?"

Josie glanced absentmindedly around the brand-new family home still smelling of fresh paint. The house was set in a recent development on the outskirts of Wichita, where every home was almost identical: large and detached with a perfectly clipped lawn. Inside, the overwhelming presence of the color beige created an insipid and characterless interior, broken up only by the occasional potted plant. But it was comfortable, with big fabric sofas and a wide-screen TV. Blade wouldn't have cared if Detective Sykes had taken them to a barn in a field. As long as he was with Josie and Archie, this was all that mattered.

When Josie didn't answer his question, Blade put a hand on her arm, and she shrank away from his touch.

"It's nice," she said, shivering slightly. "A little cold, perhaps, but the thermostat just got switched on." She walked to a heating vent in the wall and leaned against it. "There are a lot of stairs, so maybe you'd like to choose one of the downstairs rooms as your bedroom."

"Stairs are no problem for me," he said.

"Are you sure? I'm sorry. I didn't think to ask about accessibility."

"I said that stairs aren't a problem for me," he said, injecting a little annoyance into his voice. She was trying to be helpful but failing miserably. "I might sleep on the first floor, anyway," he continued. "I'd like to stay close to all the points of entry."

Josie fell silent. Something else was bothering her.

He tried to catch her eye. "What's up?"

She took her time to respond. "I'm not sure that this is a good arrangement."

"What do you mean?" Was she asking him to leave?

Josie clearly struggled to contain her tears when speaking. "I don't think it's safe for Archie to be with me right now. It's not fair to him. What if that crazy man finds me here?" She pointed to the front door. "You saw what happened on the drive over here. This guy doesn't care who gets caught up in the cross fire. Archie could end up…" She couldn't finish the sentence, and put a hand over her mouth to stop a cry from escaping.

"A detective will be stationed here twenty-four hours a day," Blade said. "And there are panic buttons in every room. Plus, I'll be here around the clock. I promise to protect our son with my own life if necessary."

She looked him straight in the eye, her green irises glinting like jade. "School starts back next week. What are you going to do then? Sit with him in class? Stand guard in the school yard at recess?"

Blade heard the hostility in her voice, but he knew it was caused by fear. "Archie is in first grade," he said. "He can take a couple of weeks off school, surely? We'll homeschool him for a while. Between the two of us, plus your dad, I think we've got all bases covered."

She sighed heavily. "We can't keep him cooped up in this house all day every day. He needs to see his friends. He needs to be a normal little boy."

Blade began to wonder what Josie was skirting around. "What are you suggesting we do? It seems like you have a plan already but are shy about sharing it."

"I think he should go stay with my aunt in Nebraska for a while. It seems like the safest option."

Blade didn't like this option at all. "How is it safer? He'll be unprotected there."

"Don't you see?" Josie replied. "My attacker isn't interested in hurting Archie. He's only interested in hurting *me*. And if he finds me here, he might target Archie to get to me. So it makes sense for us to be separated." Her voice cracked slightly. "As much as I can't bear to be parted from my little boy, I have to be sensible."

Blade could hear Archie and his granddad talking upstairs, their voices intermingled with the chirrups and whistles of Sherbet. They sounded relaxed and happy in their new environment.

"I understand your reasoning," Blade said quietly. "But I happen to think that the best thing for

Archie would be to stay with his mom. You're a family, and families should stick together at times like these."

She stood up straight. "Are you thinking of what's best for Archie or what's best for you?"

"What do you mean?"

"Well, you met your son only this morning, so I'm guessing you don't want to be parted from him." She eyeballed him, challenging him. "You don't want to send him to Nebraska because you want him here with you."

"Of course I want him here with me," Blade said, his voice rising slightly. "You've had six years to get to know our son, and I've had barely six hours." He put a hand on his heart. "It physically hurts to think of all the time I've missed out on."

"That's not my fault," Josie retorted.

"I'm not blaming you," Blade said, feeling the need to calm the situation down before they began a blazing argument. "The time I've missed with Archie is all my own fault. When I came back from Afghanistan, I should've realized there was a chance you could be pregnant. I should've talked to you instead of leaving in a hurry. I was in a bad place, and I shut you out. I'm sorrier about that than you'll ever know."

Josie leaned against the vent again. She seemed pacified by his apology.

"You'll have plenty of time to catch up with Archie and get to know him after the trial," she said. "For now, we need to focus on how to keep him safe. I'm going to call my aunt today."

Blade tried to contain the frustration that was creeping into him. "So my opinion doesn't count?" he asked. "Am I a father in name only?"

Josie's shoulders sagged. "I don't want to fight with you, Blade, but I think it's too dangerous for Archie to stay here."

"At least I can keep an eye on him if he's close to me," Blade said. "A father should be allowed to protect his son, right? There's no way I can relinquish that authority to anybody else."

She looked resigned to Blade's fierce argument. "Okay," she relented. "Then I'll ask my aunt if you can go stay with her, too. She has plenty of space, so I'm sure it won't be a problem."

Blade ran a hand down his face in exasperation. "I need to be able to protect you, too, Josie. I'd rather you and Archie were in the same place, so I can keep you *both* safe."

"I never asked you to look after me, Blade," she said coolly. "I have police detectives to do that. That's what they're trained for."

Blade raised his voice slightly. "That's what I've been trained for, too. I know how to detect danger, evade capture and protect the innocent.

And I probably know how to do it way better than a Wichita detective."

"But…" she began, before stopping.

He crossed his arms. "But what?"

"You're not a SEAL anymore. You were medically discharged, remember?"

"I'm still the same man." He looked down at his legs. "Physically there's a little less of me now, but I have the same heart I always did."

"You don't have the same body," she said. "You shouldn't be running through a hail of bullets or standing guard for hours on end. You're training for the Invictus Games, right? You can't afford to be injured. You have to protect your good leg."

He raised his eyebrows. "My good leg?"

"Yes," she said, folding her arms. "You have to take care of yourself."

He stared at her, his patience with her condescension wearing thin. "I'll take the risk."

"I'm just trying to look out for you, Blade," she said, a little more softly this time. "This is serious."

His patience finally snapped. "I know this is serious," he said. "And the risk is mine to take, not yours." His pent-up anger was threatening to burst its way out into the open, so he threw his hands up into the air and turned on his heel. "I'm done talking with you."

As he stalked away, Josie called him back. "Blade, wait."

He stopped, but kept his back to her.

"I'm sorry if I upset you," she said. "Let's not fight. I don't want Archie to see us arguing." She sighed. "I won't call my aunt today. I'll give it a few days and then reassess the situation. How does that sound?"

He let the anger flow from his body and turned around. This was progress. "It sounds like we just made our first coparenting decision. I'm happy with that arrangement."

Josie's eyes flicked everywhere but to Blade's. "Good."

Silence descended, quickly followed by awkwardness, and the huge gulf between them was evident. Neither knew how to reach out to the other, too afraid to speak for fear of igniting another disagreement.

"I'll go help Archie unpack," Josie said, running upstairs as if making a quick escape. "He might need me."

Blade watched her feet bounce up the stairs, her ballet pumps lightly brushing each step, and he wondered whether she would find every coparenting decision as difficult as that one. If so, he had a long, hard battle ahead of him.

And she not only was unwilling to share her parenting role but also continued to treat him like an invalid. Blade had come to terms with other people's misplaced offers of help, but to hear them from Josie was doubly hard. They made him sad, angry and disappointed.

He shook his head, still smarting from her comments about needing to protect his good leg. Both his legs were good. They were strong and fast, serving him well. He certainly didn't need to be cosseted and protected. Josie should have known him better than that.

But apparently, she didn't know him at all.

Josie sat on the edge of Archie's bed, watching her son play with Sherbet while her father settled into his room. The bird was out of his cage, walking along the wooden floorboards, exploring his new environment. The budgie's wings were slightly clipped, so he couldn't fly far, but he enjoyed his freedom and usually ended up in mischief somehow.

Along one wall of the bedroom was a huge mural depicting various animals that wouldn't be found living naturally side by side in the wild—lions and tigers, pandas and kangaroos, giraffes and grizzly bears—but the effect was striking and vivid. She could see why Archie loved it.

"Are you okay, Mom?" Archie asked, steering Sherbet's beak away from his Power Rangers toy. "You look like you've been crying."

Josie smiled brightly and rubbed her thumbs beneath her eyes. "I'm fine, honey." A few tears had managed to spring forth on her way up the stairs, but she had hoped her son wouldn't notice. "I'm just a little tired."

She stood and walked to the window, hoping to see Detective Pullman drive up in the car that contained her suitcase. All her clothes and toiletries were in that bag, and she didn't want to be without it. She hated to admit it, but she wanted to look her best while Blade was around. Although they were poles apart, she still felt an old attraction simmering away. Blade was as good-looking today as he was the last time she'd seen him, with sandy curls and a wide, playful smile. She admired him for pulling himself up by the bootstraps and turning his life around, but she wished he didn't look quite so handsome. It would have been much easier if he had returned to her life as a less attractive man.

She focused her attention back on her son. "Archie," she began, "how would you feel about going to stay with Aunt Susan in Nebraska for a little while?"

Josie knew that she and Blade had already discussed this issue and made a decision, but it wouldn't hurt to get Archie's feelings on the matter, would it? She ignored the sensation of disloyalty to Blade and awaited the answer.

"I want to stay with Dad," he said, continuing to play with the budgie. "I like it here, and so does Sherbet."

Archie's response was predictable. Even though he had known his dad for so little time, accepting Blade as his father came totally naturally to him, exactly as it should have been. Yet her son's words stung deeply.

"What about me?" she said with a forced laugh. "Don't you want to stay with me, too?"

"Sure," he said, jumping up to fetch Sherbet's toys. "I don't want to go to Aunt Susan's house. Her big, sloppy dog will frighten Sherbet, and she always watches boring movies where ladies cry all the time."

Josie giggled. Her aunt Susan loved old romance movies, and Archie hated them.

"Okay, honey," she said. "I just wanted to know how you felt about it."

"If I stay here with Dad, we can watch boy movies where cars turn into other stuff." Archie struck a pose, extending his arms and clenching his fists tight. "And we can pretend to be robots and fight everybody who tries to come in. It'll be awesome."

Josie bit hard on her lip. Her son had no true idea of the level of danger facing them, and she was glad of it. In his mind, he and his father could save the day simply by imagining themselves as Transformers. On arrival at the safe house, Archie had instantly torn around the place as if in a racing car, encouraging Blade to do the same. She had seen a sudden change in his behavior since Blade had shown up. In just a few hours, her son had gone from being a sweet and gentle-natured boy into a car-loving, boisterous kid. Although her own dad had tried hard to be a father figure to Archie, he was missing an essential ingredient—the energy of youth. Blade's appearance had triggered a rambunctious quality in her son, and it made her even more concerned that she was losing him. Blade was demanding an equal say in parenting, and her son had talked of little else but his father since he'd shown up. She knew it was silly, but she felt shut out.

There was a knock on the door, and Blade's voice could be heard on the other side. "Hey, anybody home?"

Josie opened the door and steered him inside. "We have to keep the door closed because Sherbet's out of his cage."

Blade looked around the room, nodding in approval. "Great bedroom, Archie. I think it might be the best in the house."

"You can share if you want," Archie said, putting the bird onto his index finger and guiding him back into the cage. "You can have the top bunk."

Josie fought hard to suppress her increasing sense of exclusion. Archie still occasionally climbed into her bed after a bad dream or during a storm. She loved being able to cuddle her son and give him the reassurance he needed, but Archie could turn to his dad for these things now. She told herself that it was natural for him to want to share his bunk beds with his dad rather than her. After all, they were just getting to know each other. But it still hurt nonetheless.

"Thanks for the offer," Blade said. "But I'll be sleeping downstairs." He tapped the side of his nose. "Kind of like a guard."

Archie's face lit up. "Cool," he said. "Can I sleep downstairs, too?"

Blade shook his head. "Only grown-ups can be guards."

Archie picked up the birdcage from the floor and held it in the air. "I'm gonna show Sherbet around the house." He looked up at his father. "Then can we play Power Rangers together?"

Blade ruffled his son's hair. "Sure, buddy."

Josie opened the door. "I'll play hide-and-seek later if you like," she suggested. "This house has loads of great places to hide."

"No, thanks, Mom," Archie said, walking out into the hallway. "I like Power Rangers better."

She tried to hide the disappointment on her face, but she wasn't quick enough.

"I'm still a novelty," Blade said. "It'll wear off soon enough." He pointed to the stairway. "Detective Pullman just arrived. He'd like to speak to us in the living room."

Josie breathed a sigh of relief and walked out into the hallway, seeing Archie walk with Sherbet up the next flight of stairs. With six bedrooms, this house would have been perfect for a game of hide-and-seek, but it looked like Archie just wasn't interested in his usual favorite game.

She heard Blade's unique footsteps behind her, one foot falling more heavily than the other. She turned to offer him her hand, but he waved it away brusquely. He had shunned all her offers of help and support, and she was a little hurt by it. It was like he was punishing her for trying to show kindness.

Detectives Pullman and Sykes were sitting in the living room, deep in a hushed and serious conversation, a pot of hot coffee in front of them. When they saw Josie come in, they rose and smiled, but she knew instantly that she had interrupted something important.

"What happened?" she asked, sitting on the couch. "Do we have to move again?"

"No," Detective Sykes said. "We have no reason to think you've been located here, but we're very concerned about your safety traveling to and from the courthouse when the trial starts on Monday."

Josie's heart skipped a beat. "Why?"

"We found the black sedan abandoned on a street in Sedgwick," Detective Pullman said. "Somebody was in a rush to escape. A notebook was left behind detailing your exact movements over the past three weeks. It shows when you leave the house in the morning, what time you eat lunch, where you go, what time you return home and even what time you switch off your lights at night. It's a perfect record of your day-to-day life."

"Someone is trying to establish a pattern," Blade said. "Looking for opportunities to strike."

"That's our assessment, also," Detective Pullman said. "It means we have to be super careful about Josie's routine, always changing it so that this person is kept guessing."

Josie felt sick. Somebody had been watching her day in and day out, and she'd had no idea. For too long, she had assumed that the menacing notes and phone calls were just empty threats, arising out of community anger at her defense of a perceived molester in their midst. But it was more than that. For three weeks, this man had been preparing to act on those threats, meticulously planning and plotting. And if the police officer hadn't been at her house this morning, he might have succeeded.

"Josie needs to have a permanent bodyguard assigned," Blade said, shifting a little closer to her. "Someone who will shadow her throughout the trial."

"I'll be acting as her bodyguard on a daily basis," Detective Sykes said. "And Detective Pullman will stay at the house with you, Archie and Tim."

"Have you undergone bodyguard training?" Blade asked. "Or advanced firearms training?"

"No, I haven't, sir," Detective Sykes replied, fixing him with steely gray eyes. "But I've been a police officer for fifteen years, and I've been a Wichita detective for six of those years. I'm used to dealing with bad guys, trust me."

"This isn't just any normal bad guy," Blade said. "This is a man who keeps painstaking records of every movement that Josie makes. He's smart. He knows that ninety percent of the work is in the preparation."

Josie shivered and leaned forward to pour a cup of coffee. Yet her hands shook so much that Blade took the pot from her hand and poured one for her. She pulled the sleeves of her cardigan over her hands and cradled the mug in her palms, allowing the warmth to seep through the fabric and act like gloves.

"I don't want to scare Josie any more than I have to, but I really think that we need a specialist assigned to protect her," Blade said. "Someone with a more advanced level of training than a police detective."

Josie knew what Blade had in mind. "Someone with training like yours, right?"

"Yes," he replied. "I'm not saying that your bodyguard needs to be a trained SEAL—"

Detective Pullman interrupted with an expression of surprise. "*You* were a SEAL, Mr. Harding?"

"Yes, I was," he replied. "Does that shock you?"

"A little. I was given very little background information on you, sir. I was only told that you are the boy's father and are a disabled veteran. I had no idea that you were in our elite forces."

"I was a navy SEAL for ten years," Blade said with a note of pride. "Until a combat injury ended my military career."

The detective nodded slowly. "I see. Well, don't worry, sir. Detective Sykes and I will take great care of you while you're under our protection."

Blade's voice was hard. "Thanks for the offer, but I don't need any protection. I'm perfectly capable of taking care of myself, and Josie, for that matter."

Detective Pullman looked confused. "I kind of assumed you'd need assistance in some areas..." He trailed off, clearly uncertain how to continue without causing embarrassment.

Blade sighed. He lifted the left leg of his jeans to reveal the prosthesis beneath. "I lost my lower left leg seven years ago. I'm actually quite fortunate, because the land-mine explosion that cost me my leg cost one of my buddies his life. At least I got out alive. Every disabled person is different, Detective Pullman, so don't be so quick to assume we're all in need of care."

Josie felt the raw emotion coming from Blade. This was clearly a touchy subject for him, and she felt a little sorry for the detective. He had meant no offense. She sat back in her chair, thankful that she had been more sensitive to Blade's situation. She treated him just the same as everybody else. He got no special treatment from her, except the occasional offer to lend a helping hand.

"I apologize," Detective Pullman said. "I take your point completely. I'm afraid we don't have access to police officers with skills as extensive as yours. The trial starts on Monday and is scheduled to last only a week or so. We simply don't have the time to recruit anybody with advanced bodyguard training."

"I'll do it," Blade said quickly.

Josie turned to him. "What? That's a crazy idea."

"What's so crazy about it?"

She didn't know where to start. "Because you shouldn't willingly put yourself in danger for me. You came here to connect with your son, not to risk your life."

He let out a short puff of air that sounded like exasperation. "I thought we discussed this already," he said. "The risk is mine to take. Besides which, I've faced way more dangerous situations than this. I came here so quickly because Archie asked me to protect you, and I intend to fulfill that promise."

Josie felt conflicted. She knew that Blade desperately wanted to act as a strong defender, yet *she* also wanted to shield *him* from harm. The public gallery could be packed, and he might have to stand on his feet for hours at a time, potentially causing him discomfort or pain, not to mention the risk of injury that she'd already pointed out to him.

"No," she said. "It's not fair. It'll be very tiring."

He regarded her for a long time, his blue eyes running across her face.

"I don't tire easily," he said flatly. "I'm not a toddler, Josie."

She put down her mug and folded her hands in her lap, saying nothing. She didn't want to fight again.

"We can't allow you to act as an official bodyguard for Josie," Detective Sykes said to Blade. "But if you wish to accompany her to the courthouse, that's your prerogative. I'll be her police escort throughout the trial, and I hope you'll allow me to do my job."

Blade held both palms in the air. "I won't interfere with your assignment, but I'll remain with Josie at all times."

"Hang on," Josie said, rising. "Don't I get a say in this?" She looked down at Blade. "You don't want Archie to go to Nebraska because you want to keep an eye on him yourself, but now you propose leaving him unprotected so you can be my shadow at the courthouse every day."

"Your son and his grandfather won't be unprotected," Detective Pullman said. "I'll be here with them constantly. We have panic buttons that link directly to the police station, so backup is only minutes away. It's the most secure environment possible."

"It makes sense, Josie," Blade said, pushing himself up from the couch. "I'd never leave

Archie if I thought it was dangerous. You need me. I know you don't believe it, but it's true."

Josie ran her hands through her hair. Her mind was racing, imagining all the scenarios and possibilities that might occur over the next week. And none were good.

"I'd like to sleep on it," she said, turning to the detectives and asking, "Are we done for now? Because I'd really like to freshen up."

"Sure," replied Detective Pullman. "We'll continue the conversation later."

With that, Josie walked from the living room, slipping her fingers through the handle of her suitcase on the way. "It's getting late," she said. "I'll ask Dad to start on dinner."

"I can do that," Blade said.

She used all her strength to heave the case up the stairs, determined to do it herself. "There's no need," she called. "Dad and I are used to sharing cooking responsibilities. We have a routine."

As she bumped the case along the carpet, she thought of how Blade had come back into her life and taken over. He had assumed the position of favored parent, and now he expected to be her personal bodyguard, monitoring her every movement.

She had tolerated his intrusion, but he had just stepped over the line. Having him so close to her each day of the trial would take a huge emotional toll. His return had reminded her of what he used to mean to her, of how she had loved him so intensely. Once upon a time he was her world. Now he was a stranger. His constant and unwavering attention made her realize what she had lost, and she didn't know how she would bear the pain.

Blade slipped his residual limb into the socket of his running prosthesis. Putting on this blade was like stepping into a pair of old, comfortable slippers. Sometimes he even forgot that the prosthesis wasn't attached to his body with skin and bone. The way that the curved artificial foot rolled smoothly from heel to toe allowed him to run hard and fast. It had been tricky at first to get the right balance between his natural leg and the blade, but with plenty of practice and determination, he'd soon mastered the action. Running had opened up a whole new world to him, full of freedom and open roads, where a disability wasn't a drawback. Running had breathed new life into his tired and hopeless spirit. And all this had happened because he had answered God's call that day on the street in Florida. God had seen that Blade was weary and heavy-laden, and He had given him rest.

With Detective Pullman locking the door behind him, Blade left the house and pulled his woolen hat down over his ears. The dark night had turned a little frosty, and he was wrapped up warmly to ward off the chill. But the chill in the air wasn't the only thing causing him discomfort. He also felt a heavy sense of menace bearing down on his new family.

He started off with a gentle jog to warm up his lungs. As long as Blade didn't cause any commotion, his daily runs wouldn't present a problem for security, and the detectives knew exactly what time to expect him back. They had even requested that he use the time to look out for anything suspicious.

He soon couldn't contain his energy and built up a good pace, feeling the blade bouncing steadily beneath him. The pressure of the day melted away with every step, and he reveled in the sensation of lithe and nimble movement. To Blade, running was as freeing as flying.

He would need to run for a long time to clear his head of the day's stress. While he had adored playing with his son all afternoon, his relationship with Josie was a little more difficult to crack. He guessed she found his sudden presence too invasive, upsetting the routines and habits that she had established over the years.

But however much she resented his intrusion, he resented hers more. Her constant desire to shield him from harm was beyond tiresome, and her reluctance to allow him to act as her body-guard was particularly hurtful. Was she worried that he wouldn't be able to cope physically? Or was she simply trying to prevent him from receiving another injury? Either way, it insulted him.

Josie needed him, whether she realized it or not. And despite his personal difficulties with her, he would step up. He was a navy SEAL, trained in close combat, surveillance and psychological warfare. And as he ran, he knew that all three of these skills would prove essential in the forthcoming battle.

FOUR

Blade smiled at his son across the breakfast table Monday morning. Archie was spooning cornflakes into his mouth, his budgie perched on his shoulder. Every now and then, the child would hand-feed the bird a cornflake and Sherbet would crunch enthusiastically, sending crumbs cascading down onto the table.

"Archie," Josie said irritably as she entered the kitchen. "You know that Sherbet isn't allowed at the dining table. It's not hygienic."

Archie's face fell. "Sorry, Mom, but I think he's scared up in my room by himself. He needs to know that everybody is safe."

Blade stood up and walked to the sink, where Josie had started to wash some cups and place them in the draining rack. Her movements were swift and absentminded, as though her thoughts weren't really on the job.

"I think Archie's transferring his feelings onto Sherbet," Blade whispered into her ear. "It's a big day today, what with the start of the trial, and he looks a little apprehensive." He glanced down at his watch, which showed 6:30 a.m. "I'm pretty sure he got up this early so that he could make sure you were okay."

Josie put down the dishcloth and turned around, leaning against the kitchen counter. She was wearing a closely fitted navy-blue suit with shiny beige heels, and her hair was tightly wound on top of her head in a neat bun. She looked every inch the confident and accomplished attorney, but her eyes betrayed a sense of unease.

"He looks okay to me," she said. "Are you sure you're not imagining things?"

"I don't think so," Blade replied. "I've known him only three days, but I can read him pretty well."

Josie clenched her teeth. He saw her jaw tighten and her nostrils flare slightly, as though trying to contain a range of emotions. He and Archie had grown incredibly close over the weekend, spending every possible minute together. At mealtimes, the seat right next to Archie was always reserved for his dad. At playtime, Archie chose soccer, wrestling or rough play with Blade and rejected his mom's suggestions of board games or baking. And at bedtime, it was Blade who Archie wanted to hear a story from. He knew it must be tough for Josie to adjust to a new regimen, especially when it meant that Blade could spot an anxiety in their son that she had missed.

"Archie," Josie said softly, going to sit at the table. "Are you okay? Are you worried about anything?"

Archie shook his head and continued to feed cornflakes to Sherbet. "I'm okay, Mom."

Josie swiveled on her chair and smiled up at Blade. It was a smile that said, *I told you so.*

But Blade knew better, and he took a seat next to his son. "How is Sherbet doing?" he asked. "Is *he* worried about anything?"

Archie put his spoon into his bowl and took the bird carefully from his shoulder, cradling it in his hand and stroking its white crested head.

"Sherbet's not doing so good," he said, keeping his eyes firmly locked on the budgie. "He knows that the big court thing starts today, and he knows that Mom will be there every day, and he thinks the bad guy might hurt her."

Josie brought her hand up to her mouth and blinked hard, clearly realizing that Blade had called it correctly after all. Archie *was* transferring his feelings onto Sherbet because he didn't want to let his mother down by being scared and needy. She gently pulled her son from his chair and guided him onto her lap, wrapping her arms around his torso and holding him close. Archie nestled into his mother, cradling the bird in both hands.

"Why don't you tell Sherbet that your dad is going to be Mom's very own special bodyguard?" Blade said.

As he spoke these words, he saw Josie stiffen, as if she wasn't really on board with this plan. She had already agreed to it, but not with enthusiasm. Archie, however, received the news with delight, straightening his back and smiling broadly.

"Really? You're Mom's bodyguard?"

"Absolutely, kiddo," Blade said, giving his son a soft chin punch. "We didn't want to tell you over the weekend, but I'll be going with your mom to the courthouse every single day, and nobody will have any chance to hurt her while I'm around."

"Every day?" Archie asked. "Even today?"

Blade looked at the clock on the wall. Josie would be leaving in a half hour to go to the Wichita courthouse. She wanted to be there early on this first day of the trial. He had felt the tension radiating from her all morning.

"Yup," Blade replied with a smile. "I'll be there today, and you'll stay here with Granddad and Detective Pullman."

"Detective Pullman says I can call him Dave,"

Archie said, visibly relaxing. "We're friends now. He's awesome at Jenga."

Blade laughed. "Well, Dave is in charge until we get back this evening, okay? And then you and I can play ball in the yard."

Josie cleared her throat. "What about me?" She was projecting a playful voice, but he distinctly heard a hurt edge to the words. "Don't I get to play, too?"

"Sure," he said. "I just figured that you'd have a ton of work to do this evening."

"Nothing is more important than playing with my son," she said strongly. "I'll find the time."

Archie hopped off his mother's lap and headed for the door, seemingly appeased by the news that his dad would be acting as her capable bodyguard.

"Sherbet feels better now," he said. "I'll go put him back in his cage." He turned around as he seemed to remember something important. "School starts tomorrow." He smiled hopefully. "Do I get to stay home?"

"Yes," Josie said as she stood up. "But it's only for a little while, and I've arranged for your teacher to send some homework via email, so it's not a vacation."

Archie brought Sherbet's face close to his. "Did you hear that?" he whispered to the bird. "We get to stay home. And we don't have to go to Aunt Susan's house." He kissed Sherbet's beak. "Yippee."

Josie shook her head. "It's amazing how a child's attitude can change in a heartbeat."

She sat back down, and Blade put a hand on top of hers. Her fingers were icy cold. "Are you all right? You look nervous."

"I'm scared to death," she said, sliding her hand from beneath his. "This is the biggest case I've ever handled, and I don't want to let Norman down."

"You'll be just fine," he said reassuringly. "I know you will."

She took a deep breath and clasped her hands together on the fabric of her blouse pulled taut across her stomach. "To be honest, the trial isn't the only thing that's weighing on my mind."

"It isn't?"

She fixed him with her beautiful pale eyes. "I feel like I'm losing Archie to you," she said. "You're the only person he wants now. I'm redundant."

"That's not true," he said with a shake of the head. "It's only natural for Archie to be infatuated with me at first. He's making up for lost time. It won't last."

"But what if it does last?" she said. "What if he decides that you're the most important person in the world? What if you go back to North

Carolina and Archie asks to go with you?" She placed the tip of her index finger in the corner of her eye to flick away the moisture. "It could happen."

Blade couldn't help but laugh. "You're overthinking this, Josie."

She cut him off angrily. "Don't tell me what I'm overthinking," she snapped. "I see my son drifting further and further away every day."

"But it's been three days," he said. "You can't judge this situation on just three days."

"Three days will turn into three weeks and into three months and then into three years." She took a deep breath. "If I don't do something about it now, then I may be too late."

Blade moved his chair closer to hers. He caught her delicate scent that reminded him of a candy shop. "Too late for what, Josie?"

She looked down at her lap. "Too late to keep him with me," she said quietly. "Like I said, he might decide he wants to go live with you, and a family court could rule that it's in his best interest to be with his dad." She brought her hands over her face. "Oh, I don't know. I never anticipated this."

Blade put a hand on her shoulder. She flinched. "I would never, ever take our son away from you. You should know me better than that."

She fixed him with another stare. "Do I know

you, Blade? I feel like I don't know a single thing about you anymore."

"Listen to me," he said, taking her hand. "I haven't come here to snatch Archie away. I understand why you're afraid, but you have no need to be. I have no hidden agenda or ulterior motive. I'm here to build a relationship with the son I never knew I had and make sure you both stay safe. That's all."

Josie swallowed hard. Her emotions looked to be threatening to overwhelm her. He couldn't believe that she thought he was capable of taking her son away from her. That was the last thing on his mind.

"It's a big day, and you'll need all your strength to make it through," he said. "Would it help if we started off today with a prayer?"

A smile passed across her lips, so he took her other hand and clasped them together in his.

"Dear Heavenly Father…"

Josie strode confidently along the path leading to the Sedgwick County Courthouse in Wichita. She was flanked on either side by Blade and Detective Sykes, and they led her quickly past a small gathering of newspaper photographers who were trying to get a perfect shot of the public defender representing the most hated man in Sedgwick County.

"Step aside," Detective Sykes ordered, making a sweeping gesture with her hand. Her expression was tense, and she jerked her head quickly, looking in all directions for the presence of possible danger.

The photographers moved away from the path, allowing Josie to walk through the entrance of the dull gray building. With several floors, plenty of windows and no ornate features, the courthouse always reminded her of a big, ugly shoe box. She was a regular visitor there, handling many more cases than just Norman Francis's, but none had attracted as much attention as this one.

Once inside, they were ushered through security, and Josie saw Blade hand his weapon to the guard. She knew it would be difficult for him to act as her bodyguard while being unarmed. Yet in spite of this, she still found herself surprisingly calmed by his strong presence next to her. Much as she didn't want to rely on him, his self-assurance and commanding aura were comforting. But she reminded herself that Blade wasn't the same man as he was years ago. He was now physically challenged, and she couldn't expect him to jeopardize himself for her. She was allowing Blade to accompany her because he was insistent, but if danger struck, she intended to take care of herself.

She caught sight of the trial's prosecuting attorney, Allan Sanders, rushing down the inner staircase, glasses askew, tie off-center, wild gray hair sticking out in all directions. In spite of his disheveled appearance, Sanders was one of the most ruthless and determined attorneys Josie had ever known. And he desperately wanted to win this case. He had been on a losing streak lately, failing to secure successful prosecutions in a number of high-profile cases. She had heard plenty of rumors that he might be about to lose his position as state prosecutor, so this case gave Sanders the opportunity to redeem himself and be the shining star.

Josie tried to avoid his eye as she entered the tiled hallway of the courthouse, which was quiet and empty at the early hour. But there was no escaping his gaze, and he came rushing over, beaming from ear to ear.

"Ah, Josie," he said, clasping her hand firmly. "You're making a nice, early start, I see. A wise choice considering the difficulty you're facing in defending this repugnant man."

Josie drew her hand away from his. "A defendant is considered innocent until proven guilty, Allan. You, of all people, should know that."

Sanders rolled his eyes. "I think this case is pretty watertight. You should've taken the deal when it was offered." His gaze slid over to Blade and Detective Sykes. "And I see you've brought along some reinforcements."

Josie didn't much feel like being civil to Allan Sanders, but her manners prevented her from revealing it.

"Allan," she said, gesturing first to Blade and then to Detective Sykes. "This is former navy SEAL Blade Harding and police detective Carly Sykes. They'll be ensuring that I remain safe for the duration of the trial."

"Ah, yes, I've heard about the threats you've been receiving," Sanders said, shaking hands. "It's a terrible state of affairs. I only hope it doesn't affect your performance in the courtroom. I must admit, I think you're incredibly brave to continue with this trial. I'm sure the public defender's office would assign a good replacement attorney if you bowed out."

"I've worked on this case for eighteen months already," Josie snapped. "I want to see justice served."

Sanders pinched his lips together. "How very noble of you." He glanced over his shoulder. "In that case, I would imagine that you're eager to get on with business. Mr. Francis is waiting for you in meeting room five."

"Norman is here already?"

"The police escorted him through the back entrance a few minutes ago," Sanders replied.

"They're concerned that we may see some protesters here today who object to their tax dollars being spent on defending a child abductor."

"What?" she exclaimed. "Are you serious?"

A smug smile passed Sanders's lips. "Emotions are running high, Josie. Who knows what will happen?" he said, turning on his heel and walking away, the clipping sound of his shiny shoes echoing on the tiled floor.

"Oh, that man infuriates me," Josie muttered, feeling Blade's arm curl around her shoulder. "He's not going to make it easy for me in court, that's for sure."

"Who cares what he does in court?" Blade said. "He's trying to unsettle you because he feels threatened by you. He knows you can win this case."

She leaned into Blade's firm torso, using him as a resting post while she gathered her thoughts and strength. His athletic figure, tall and wide, felt like a shield, and his soothing words were just what she needed to hear at that moment. Then she remembered that her extra weight bearing down on him was likely putting a strain on his leg, so she straightened up and apologized.

"Let's get you to meeting room five," Detective Sykes said. She turned to Blade. "I'm afraid you won't be able to accompany us, Mr. Harding, so I suggest you go take a seat in the public gallery."

Josie stepped away from Blade, instantly feeling cold at the removal of his body warmth. "Enjoy the show," she said with a weak smile. "Thanks for coming."

"Nothing would stop me from being here," he said solemnly. "I hope you trust me to watch over you today."

"I do," she said, yet she guessed he heard the hesitation in her voice. She couldn't shake her concern for him.

Blade brushed a hand down her arm as she turned to walk away. It was intended as a gesture of reassurance, but it served only to highlight the awkwardness between them. They skittered around each other like cats on a roof, neither sure where each other's territory began and ended. She was suspicious and afraid of everything he did, worried about the repercussions it would have on her closeness with Archie. She would never stand in the way of Blade forming a solid bond with Archie, but that didn't mean she had to like it.

"Knock 'em dead," Blade said, backing away. "You'll be great."

Josie sensed him watching her as she headed for the meeting room, keeping eyes on her until she was out of sight. Then she tried to push all thoughts of Blade from her mind. Today was the beginning of the hardest few days of her life. Somebody wanted to stop her in her tracks, and she had to summon all her courage to overcome that threat.

A man's reputation and freedom hung in the balance, and she was his only hope.

Josie sat tensely in the courtroom, listening to Allan Sanders present his opening statement to the jury. The jury selection process had been grueling, and she and Sanders had clashed several times regarding individual candidates, but she was content with the final jurors chosen: seven women and five men. Now that these twelve people were in place, the argument and presentation of evidence could begin. And Sanders was coming out fighting, telling the jurors that this child, Lisa Brown, could be *their* child, fortunate to be rescued from Norman's house unharmed. He repeatedly referred to her as *little Lisa*, constantly reminding the courtroom of her vulnerability and defenselessness. It was a cheap trick, but it was effective.

As Sanders spoke, Norman kept his head bowed, as if afraid to look up and catch anyone's eye. She had told him time and time again that it was important to make eye contact with the jury, allowing them the opportunity to see his honest reactions. He had nothing to hide, so he shouldn't act as if he did. He also insisted on wearing his large overcoat in the courtroom, despite Josie gently trying to persuade him not to. She knew that he was ashamed of his disability, but he was playing into the hands of the prosecution. He perfectly fitted the stereotype of a bogeyman, with his oversize coat and hunched shoulders. But he was scared and intimidated by the courtroom drama and wasn't dealing with it well.

Josie admitted to herself that she was more than a little scared by the prospect that her attacker could have sneaked into the public gallery somehow to observe her, to watch for every little moment of weakness, reveling in her discomfort. She feared for Norman, yet she also feared for herself. She felt sick.

She glanced behind her and saw Detective Sykes sitting in the front row, alert and watchful. Farther back, in the very last row, was Blade, his head and shoulders easily visible above all others. His arms were folded, and he was sitting very still, a determined expression on his face.

As she ran her gaze over the many people in the gallery, her eyes came to rest on a strangely familiar one. It was a man wearing a baseball cap pulled down low over his eyeglasses. His big, bushy beard hid his face well, but as she locked eyes with him, a moment of familiarity passed between them, and he pulled his cap even lower, sinking in his chair. How did she know this man? The courtroom was full, with standing room only, and he was likely to be a member of the community, interested in following the details of the trial like everybody else. So why did the hairs on the back of her neck stand upright? Why did her stomach swirl with anxiety? And why did this man seem to want to hide from her eyes? It seemed unlikely that he would have been permitted to enter the gallery wearing that hat, because head wear was forbidden in the court. He must have brought it in with him and put it on once he was seated.

Josie turned back around, realizing that she was losing the thread of Sanders's opening statement. She needed to be fully engaged with the courtroom, not worried about who might be in the gallery behind her. She took deep, steadying breaths, forcing her heart rate to slow. Pulling her shoulders back and sitting bolt upright, she concentrated on each and every word being said. Finally it was her turn to stand and present the opening statement of the defense.

"Ladies and gentlemen of the jury," she began. "Many people are calling my client a monster…"

That was as far as she managed to get. A huge shout echoed around the courtroom. The public gallery erupted in chaos, with people standing to hurl abusive comments at Norman, pointing fingers and raising fists. A young man tried to force his way to the front of the court, only to be grabbed by a security officer, assisted by Detective Sykes, who leaped from her chair like a lightning bolt. The judge called for order. Norman darted his head from left to right like a startled rabbit. And in the middle of it all, Allan Sanders smiled, as if immensely enjoying the commotion.

Josie's gaze immediately returned to the man in the baseball hat, who had stayed in his seat, studying the scene, turning his head almost robotically, seemingly scrutinizing each person, each exit, each window and, above all else, scrutinizing her.

She flicked her eyes to Blade. He had clearly been watching her every move and had already noticed her suspicion of the bearded man in the third row.

Blade stood, pointed to the man and mouthed the word. "Him?"

Josie nodded, and Blade began to make his way from his seat. Yet the man in the hat was one step ahead. He had risen and approached a security officer, whispering into his ear, before pointing to Blade and quickly leaving the courtroom. The officer nodded curtly and approached

Blade. Blade tried to sidestep to follow the man from court, but the officer pushed against his shoulders, ordering him to stop. Whatever the bearded man had whispered into the officer's ear, it clearly had the desired effect. Blade was now under suspicion as a troublemaker.

As the melee died down, the judge's patience appeared to wear thin, and he warned all spectators that any disorder would result in their immediate removal from the court. As several people were led away, still shouting, Josie tried to reassure Norman that this would be unlikely to happen again.

"I did warn you that public feeling was running high," Sanders said, leaning sideways in his seat. "And who can blame them?"

"I didn't ask you for your opinion, Allan," Josie snapped, turning away from him and focusing on Blade, who was patted down by the officer, had his ID checked and then was questioned. He looked to be calm, polite and deferential in response, defusing the situation perfectly. The officer allowed him to retake his seat, and Josie breathed a sigh of relief.

"Ladies and gentlemen," the judge said loudly. "I apologize for this disgraceful intrusion into my courtroom. Now that the offending protesters have been removed, let us resume proceedings." He looked at Josie. "Counselor, would you please continue?"

Josie was momentarily panicked. She had lost her train of thought, and she riffled through her papers to pick it up again. Allan Sanders sat back in his chair, his face etched with self-satisfaction. Seconds ticked by in agonizing silence.

"Counselor?" the judge questioned. "Are you able to continue?"

"Yes...yes, Your Honor," she stammered. "I'm sorry for the delay."

She briefly closed her eyes, lifted her heart up to God, calmed herself and took solace in a quick prayer. When she opened her eyes again, she couldn't stop herself from briefly glancing over the faces in the gallery, desperately searching out the man in the hat. She knew he was gone, but he had left some kind of invisible yet indelible mark on the room.

She took a deep breath and lifted her head high, projecting her voice across the court. "Ladies and gentlemen of the jury..."

Blade waited anxiously for Josie, pacing the corridor outside the room where she was running through the day's events with Norman. After the opening statements had finally been completed, the prosecution had called two of Norman's neighbors to the stand. Both witnesses testified that they saw Norman smiling at, and talking to, Lisa Brown over the fence around her yard during the course of the day. Although this certainly wasn't proof of his guilt, Blade saw some of the jurors watching Norman intently, taking in his odd appearance, no doubt wondering why this disheveled and gray-haired old man would be taking an interest in a three-year-old girl. Josie's cross-examination could have only a limited effect, as Norman freely admitted speaking in a friendly manner to the child. However, these two witnesses weren't the defense's main concern. Tomorrow the star witness, Janice Weeks, would be called to present her testimony. According to Josie, Miss Weeks had the capability to damage the defense immeasurably.

Blade had spent much of the day scanning the building for the man in the baseball hat, the man who had clearly spooked Josie. When the guy left the courtroom during the commotion caused by protesters, a security officer had prevented Blade from following after this same man had falsely informed him that Blade was carrying a weapon. Once he had been searched and his ID checked, the officer apologized and radioed the reception desk to prevent the suspect from leaving. But it was too late. He had made a quick getaway. The door in front of Blade opened and Josie appeared, her eyes weary and tired. But she stood erect and poised, holding a briefcase in one hand and letting the other loosely rest on her hip. Her navy-blue suit was showing a few creases after the busy day, and strands of her hair were beginning to escape her neatly pinned bun, but he had never seen her looking more beautiful. He felt a tug at his heart and suppressed the sensation. Blade had once loved Josie with every fiber in his body, but that was long ago. It was only the existence of Archie that had taken him back into her life. The bond they had shared was long since dead, and he now had a new passion: running. Running had already filled many years of loneliness and would probably fill many more.

"The police tell me that there are some protesters out front," Josie said nervously, peering around the corner to the large exit doors. "So we'll be escorted out the back door. Norman has already left with a police officer."

"I'm guessing the protesters are part of the same group who disrupted the trial this morning?" Blade asked.

"Correct," she replied. "The community is pretty angry that tax dollars are being used to fund Norman's defense, so there's widespread sympathy for those people who got kicked out by the judge today. They've been drumming up extra supporters on social media, so their numbers have grown."

"Surely the public can't deny a man a right to a fair trial?" Blade asked incredulously. "Everybody gets equal treatment no matter what they're alleged to have done."

Josie sighed heavily. "The local newspaper ran an article this morning claiming that Norman has thousands of dollars hidden away in a bank account that he failed to disclose to the court. I just became aware of it, so we weren't able to issue a denial in time. People now assume that Norman is not only a child abductor but also a fraud, using the public defender to avoid spending his own money."

"What evidence does the newspaper have to support the allegation?" Blade asked. "That's a pretty serious accusation to make."

"A clerk at a local bank says that Norman holds an account with a ninety-thousand-dollar balance. She gave bank statements to a journalist to back up the claim."

Blade was confused. "Doesn't a judge have the authority to summon the bank records of a defendant before allocating a public defender?"

"Yes," Josie replied. "But the judge took Norman at his word. Norman supplied the court with a very detailed account of his income and expenses. He made it clear that he has no money, and the judge believed him."

Blade steered Josie close to the wall as two security officers walked past, tense looks on their faces. "Is it true? Does Norman have that kind of money stashed away?"

Josie let out a high laugh. "Absolutely not. Nobody selects the public defender by choice. It's the last resort for most people."

Blade smiled. Josie was missing a vital point. "That all depends on whether the public defender is *you*. You'd probably be the first choice for plenty of people."

"It's nice of you to say that, but it's not true. If Norman had ninety thousand dollars, he'd have used it to hire a private attorney."

"So, is the clerk lying?" Blade asked. "Or is it a mistake?"

"I don't know," Josie replied with a weary voice. "I just don't know. It's possible that there's another Norman Harold Francis in Sedgwick who is the true account holder, or it could be a malicious attempt by somebody to set him up and cause us trouble."

Josie jumped slightly as Detective Sykes appeared at her side and touched her arm.

"Sorry," the detective said. "I didn't mean to startle you. We're leaving now, but I'm afraid that the protesters have realized we're using the back entrance to avoid them, so they've spread themselves around the building." She looked solemnly at Josie. "Stay close to me at all times."

"That goes for me, too," Blade said, positioning himself on Josie's opposite side and curling an arm around her shoulder.

Blade heard the protesters before he saw them. As he approached the back door, their shouts and chants were clearly audible, and he guessed that they were small in number but loud in voice. He was right. Only around ten people were standing on the other side of the door, but they quickly tripled in number when those from the front of the building joined them, encouraged by the rise in noise. With some carrying signs, they began to chant "Make him pay," which Blade assumed had a double meaning for Norman.

He pulled Josie even tighter. Some of the protesters began to jostle them, pushing hard against Blade's arm, pulling at his sweatshirt. He began to grow concerned that they might be overwhelmed.

Detective Sykes yelled out an order. "Stay back! Or you'll all be arrested."

Blade suddenly felt Josie's hand grip his tightly. "Blade," she said. Her eyes were wide with fear. "It's the guy in the baseball hat. He has a gun."

Blade spun around. "Where is he?"

Josie tried to reply, but the crack of a gunshot drowned out her words, and the crowd erupted in screams of terror.

FIVE

Josie fell to the ground, knocked down by the numerous people rushing around her. Her knees scraped on the gravelly path, and a stinging sensation spread quickly across her skin. Blade helped her to her feet, shielding her with his own body, and she darted her eyes from person to person, searching out the man in the hat.

The crowd of protesters was panicked, scattering in all directions, yelling out in fear and alarm. Security officers came rushing from the courthouse, guns drawn, desperate to find the armed man. Only one single shot had been fired, but more could come.

"Where is he?" Blade yelled above the noise. "Do you still see him?"

"No," she replied, breathlessly. "He's gone." Blade was holding her tight. She felt constrained, and her chest was hurting. She pointed to the path that led away from the courthouse. "He was standing in the parking lot."

"Remind me what he looks like," Detective Sykes said, motioning for two security officers to come and assist her. She then handed some keys to Blade. "Get Josie in the car immediately."

"Yankees baseball cap, big, bushy beard and black-framed glasses," Josie said, visualizing the man sitting in the gallery. "But I'm pretty sure he's gone."

Detective Sykes, however, had other ideas. "I think I see him." She raised her weapon and shouted, "Stop right where you are!"

Josie turned around, spotting a man in a Yankees hat, cowering against the wall of the court building. But the clothes were wrong, and this guy had a neatly trimmed beard rather than a big, bushy one. It wasn't the same man.

Detective Sykes's shout had spooked the crowd, sending them into a renewed panic. Josie found herself being pushed and elbowed as the people began to run once more. Clutching her briefcase tightly to her chest, she lost her footing and started to fall. Yet she didn't hit the concrete, because Blade scooped her off her feet and began to walk through the running figures toward the parking lot. He carried her as if she were as light as a bird, but she knew she must be placing a strain on his prosthesis. She stiffened her back and he placed her on her feet, taking her hand and leading her swiftly to the SUV.

Only once she was safely inside the car did she let out a long exhalation of relief.

"That's not our guy," she said, watching Detective Sykes cuffing the ashen-faced man in the Yankees hat. "It's the same baseball hat, but unless he trimmed his beard, removed his glasses and changed his clothes since this morning, it's not him."

Blade steered her chin away from the window. "Forget the guy," he said gently. "Are you okay? You're not hurt, are you?"

She put her palms briefly on her knees, where her panty hose were ripped and bloodied skin was visible. "Not seriously," she said. "It's just a few scratches."

"We'll get you out of here as soon as possible," he said, opening the door and stepping out. "I'll just check the car for any planted devices before we start it up."

Once the door was closed, Josie allowed her head to fall heavily into her hands, and she let out a stifled sob. She was way more terrified than she had admitted to Blade. Hearing the shot ring out had caused her mind to go into sudden overdrive, picturing her funeral, imagining Archie being forced to grow up as a motherless child. In a split second, she had contemplated how her son would cope without her. If anything happened to her, she guessed that custody of Archie would automatically be granted to his father. But could she trust Blade to take their child under his protection and care for him every day? She just didn't know. Blade was besotted with his son right now, but would the novelty wear off? He had abandoned her once already, severing all ties and leaving her utterly alone. If he could do that to *her*, could he also do the same thing to his son?

Detective Sykes opened the driver's door, causing Josie to jump in surprise. She had been lost in a world of her own morbid thoughts.

"The man in the baseball hat has agreed to accompany officers to the station to answer some questions," the detective said. "So I'll take you home before joining them at the Wichita Police Department."

"It's not the guy from the courtroom," Josie said flatly.

"I guessed as much after we didn't find a gun on him. But he says that he saw the shooter run away from the scene, so we'll get a witness statement from him. It looks like the shooter fired randomly into the air. I don't think he was trying to hit a target. He was trying to create confusion and chaos, probably to frighten you." The detective leaned into the back and patted

Josie's hand. "We'll beef up our security, so please don't worry that something like this will happen again."

Josie didn't feel the need to reply. She *knew* something like this would happen again. She was certain of it.

"You told me at lunchtime that you recognize this man from somewhere," Detective Sykes continued. "So we'll try and figure out how you might know his face."

Josie let her head fall back onto the headrest. How on earth would she now find the time to play with her son? Her whole life was being consumed by this thug and his cruel game of cat and mouse.

Blade slid into the seat next to her. "We're all clear," he said to Detective Sykes. "Nothing has been tampered with."

The detective nodded and started up the engine, taking the car away from the scene and out onto the highway. The protesters were being quickly dispersed by security officers, while the police began a search of the area, trying to seek out the culprit who had struck fear into everyone's hearts.

Blade fastened his belt and then turned his body to face Josie. He looked to be totally relaxed and at ease, the opposite of her.

"Don't look so worried," he said quietly. "I

know it was a pretty nasty shock back there, but you were well protected the whole time. From now on, we'll ask the police to form a barrier between you and the protesters. The shooter obviously hid himself among the crowd."

She pulled her pencil skirt down awkwardly to hide her scrapes. She felt like a schoolgirl who had skinned her knees rather than a professional attorney. She hated this feeling of vulnerability and wished that she had been able to stride away from court confidently and proudly, rather than in the arms of her ex-fiancé. She had vowed that she wouldn't place Blade in danger, yet she had broken that vow within a matter of hours.

"Hey," Blade said, ducking his head to make eye contact with her. "Are you sure you're okay?"

She inhaled a long breath through her nose and exhaled through her mouth. "I just got a vision of what life might be like for Archie if this guy managed to kill me."

Blade shook his head. "He's *not* going to succeed."

"You don't know that, not for sure. If he's brazen enough to come into the courtroom, then I don't think a few extra police officers are going to stop him."

She watched the wet streets of Wichita pass them by, the ground glistening from recent rainfall. Dusk was falling, and she imagined Archie settling down to watch his favorite TV show, probably with Sherbet perched on his shoulder.

"What would happen to Archie if I wasn't here anymore?" she asked in a whisper.

Blade looked to be searching her eyes. "Is that a question you want me to answer, or are you just thinking out loud?"

"I want you to answer," she replied. "I need to know."

"Well," he said, taking her hand and holding it firmly, "I think you're worrying unnecessarily, but I would take care of Archie in that circumstance."

"It's a big commitment," she said. "It's not easy being a full-time parent, and it's incredibly time-consuming…"

Blade cut her off. "I'm his father. I'd do whatever it takes."

"Would you take him back to North Carolina with you?" She moistened her lips with her tongue. Her mouth was dry and her throat scratchy. "Or would you move to Sedgwick?"

Blade sighed. "It's crazy to be talking about something that is never going to happen."

She raised her eyes to meet his. "It's not crazy to plan for my son's future." She heard the hard edge to her voice and softened it. "Before you came back into our lives, it was much simpler. My will states that I want my father to be

Archie's guardian in the event of my death. It's always been important for me to know that Archie's future is secure." She withdrew her hand from his and laced her fingers together. "But now it's different. If I died, you would be awarded custody if you wanted it. You'd be free to do what you wanted."

Blade's forehead creased. "I'm not sure what you imagine I'd do in that situation, Josie, but you seem to have a fairly low opinion of me. Do you think that I'd take Archie away from his home, his friends and his family without a second thought?"

"Would you?" she asked.

His answer was quick. "No."

"So, what would you do?"

"I don't know."

Josie let out a short exhalation. This wasn't a satisfying answer. She was getting nowhere.

"What this really boils down to," said Blade solemnly, "is your difficulty in letting go of your status as a single parent. It's hard for you to accept that I get to make the same decisions as you regarding Archie's welfare." He smiled weakly. "I'm guessing that you want to give me exact instructions on what you'd like me to do if you weren't around anymore. Am I right?"

She couldn't argue with this statement. "I just want to make sure you would do the right thing."

"But your version of the right thing might be different from mine," he argued. "You can't control how I parent. You have to let me make my own choices as a father and try not to second-guess me."

These were hard words for Josie to hear. He was articulating all her worst fears. What if Blade made poor choices? What if he took Archie camping and let him wander too close to the water? Or allowed him to ride his bike without a helmet?

Blade seemed to be able to read her thoughts. "I'd step up. I'm not a careless person, and I take my responsibilities very seriously."

"But there's so much you don't know about Archie," she said, her mind whirring. "Like, he's scared of horses. And he gets very agitated when walking over bridges, so I sing songs to calm him down." She reached into the collar of her blouse to touch the label. "And I have to cut the labels out of all his clothes because they bother him. I know these things may sound insignificant to you, but they're important to Archie, and you might accidentally do something to upset him or hurt his feelings."

Blade laughed. It was a rich, throaty laugh that came from deep inside. "He doesn't need to be wrapped in cotton, Josie. He's not a baby."

Josie bristled at this comment. "Do you think I coddle him?"

"A little."

She hadn't expected him to be truthful, and his words stung.

"I don't blame you for wanting the very best for our son," Blade continued. "I think you're a fantastic mom, and Archie is a fantastic kid. But I'm not the same as you. I do things differently. I'll let Archie climb right to the top of the jungle gym or swim in the deep end of the pool."

Josie knit her eyebrows together. Blade had just told her he wasn't a careless person, yet these things he had mentioned were totally careless and could put Archie's well-being at risk.

He clearly saw the unhappy expression on her face. "But I'll be right there to make sure he's always safe from harm. You can't protect children from every eventuality. You can only teach them how to deal with problems when they arise and let them have a little more independence as they grow."

"I'm not sure I agree," said Josie, her concern growing. "It's my job to protect Archie from as many things as I can until he's grown up and able to look after himself."

"But don't you see?" said Blade. "Unless you teach him how to cope with dangerous situations while he's young, he'll never be able to handle it as an adult."

Josie shook her head. "That's easy enough to say while we're sitting in a warm and safe car, but what if you're not able to get to him fast enough in the pool or the park? What if you're not wearing your prosthesis and you can't reach him in time? What if—"

Blade raised a hand. "Do you think my disability makes me less able to take care of Archie?"

"No, not at all," she said quickly. "I didn't mean for you to take it the wrong way."

"I don't think I took it the wrong way," Blade said calmly. "I think I took it the exact way it was intended."

Josie closed her eyes briefly. She was making a big mess of this. She didn't want Blade to feel bad, but neither did she want him to flirt with danger when it came to Archie's safety.

"I apologize," she said, not really meaning it. She thought that Blade was a little touchy on the subject of his disability, and his taking offense was unwarranted. "I just wanted to make sure we were on the same page in parenting terms, but apparently we're not. Can we start this conversation over again?"

Blade turned to look out the window. "Actually, I'd prefer not to talk for a while. You've given me a lot to think about." He looked at her in the reflected glass. "Are you sure you're okay after that shooting incident?"

"I'm fine," she replied tersely. "Thanks for asking."

All thoughts of her attacker had now been banished from Josie's mind, replaced by an even greater worry. She had wanted reassurance from Blade that he would take care of their son if anything bad happened to her, but his words had given her no comfort. If her attacker succeeded in terminating her, Blade would have free rein to parent Archie any way he liked. He could take Archie kayaking down white-water rapids without a life vest if he wanted. And she would have no way to curtail this kind of recklessness.

There was only one thing she could do: she must ensure that her attacker did *not* succeed. She simply had to stay alive for the sake of her precious son.

Later that night, Blade loaded up the dishwasher while Tim made a pot of coffee. Blade and Josie had returned to the safe house to be greeted by a wonderful aroma of roast chicken, cooked by Archie and his granddad in preparation for their return from court. When Blade had walked into the hallway, Archie had instantly run and jumped into his father's arms, but Blade quickly passed him along to Josie. He guessed that she needed to wrap her arms around her son after the day she'd had.

Their conversation in the car told him just how difficult she was finding this process of adjustment. The sudden presence of another parent in her family had totally changed the dynamic. Josie no longer had the final say on Archie's future, and it was clear that she wasn't coping well with this. Her insensitive comment about him potentially failing to rescue Archie from danger because of his prosthesis had really hurt deeply.

Despite their tense verbal exchanges, Blade still couldn't help old feelings stirring up inside whenever he looked at Josie. Her blazing eyes and ruby-red mouth were her most dangerous weapons, and she used them frequently to get her point firmly across. Yet Blade was never cowed by her. Far from it—he admired and respected her for her strength and confidence, remembering exactly why he fell in love with her in the first place. But her attitude toward his disability continued to be a sticking point between them. She was like a bull in a china shop, making the kind of clumsy comments that he knew were meant to be helpful but only highlighted her lack of understanding.

"Dad, can we play ball in the yard?" Archie asked, carrying the last plate from the table.

Blade glanced out the window, where night had fallen.

"It's too dark to go outside, buddy, but why don't we play something indoors?" He looked at Josie, who was poring over some documents at the kitchen table, seemingly lost in thought. She had cleaned her wounds and changed into a sweatshirt and jeans. Although her eyes were on the paper, they were staring right through the page. "How about hide-and-seek?" he asked. "What do you say, Josie?"

She looked up, startled. "Huh?"

"Do you want to play hide-and-seek with me and Archie?"

Archie jumped up and down on the spot. "Me first. Me first."

Josie picked up her papers and slipped them into her briefcase, smiling. "Sounds like a great idea. Archie, your dad and I will give you one whole minute to hide."

Archie didn't need telling twice. He tore out of the room, and Blade heard small feet pounding on the stairs as he ran like the wind.

Blade went to sit next to Josie at the table just as Detective Sykes poked her head around the corner. After dropping them at the safe house, the detective had immediately gone to the Wichita station to interview the man in the baseball cap. She had been gone for a couple of hours.

"I smell coffee," she said with a smile. "Any chance of a cup?"

"Sure," Tim replied, reaching for mugs on the shelf. "We saved some dinner for you. It's in the oven."

"Thanks," she said. "It's been a long day and I need a good, hot meal." She sat at the table. "Josie, do you think we could talk after I've eaten? I have some mug shots for you to look through. You might recognize the shooter from the courthouse today."

"No problem," Josie said, watching her father carry a plate from the oven with an oven mitt. "You go ahead and eat, and I'll be back in ten minutes, okay?"

The detective picked up her fork. "Perfect."

Blade then followed Josie out into the hallway and watched her flit up the carpeted stairs, sure-footed and bouncy. His gait was a little more cumbersome when climbing stairs but not much slower than hers. He was pleased that the mood was lifting a little. They all needed to feel like a normal, happy family, instead of a family in hiding. Archie had no idea about the shooting incident earlier in the day, and Blade and Josie had jointly decided not to tell him. That was one thing they had agreed on, at least.

"I'm coming for you, Archie," Josie called out in a teasing tone once she got to the second-floor landing. She pointed to the next flight of stairs and turned to Blade. "I'll go look on the top floor, and you take this one."

"The loser has to make breakfast in the morning," he said, jogging to the bedroom at the end of the hallway.

She laughed. "It's a deal." He glanced back to see her taking the stairs two at a time, calling out, "I'd like bacon and eggs, please."

Blade started hunting beneath beds, in closets and behind drapes. He then realized that he was enjoying himself more than he had in a very long time. The game seemed to have brought out a playful side in both him and Josie, allowing them to forget the stress of the day and focus on what was really important. At this moment, he truly felt part of a real family. Yet he knew it was all make-believe. After the trial was over and danger passed, he would return to North Carolina and become a part-time dad, snatching weekends with his son in between his training sessions for the Invictus Games. He wondered how Josie might react if he were to relocate to Kansas. Would she see it as an encroachment on her turf? He didn't know what to do.

Archie was clearly very good at hiding, because a ten-minute search proved fruitless. He was nowhere to be found, and Josie came padding down the stairs with a confused look on her face.

"Where did he go?" she asked. "I don't see him anywhere." She couldn't conceal the panic written on her face. "You don't think someone was lying in wait, do you?" She spun around, looking in every direction. "Did the detectives check the house today?"

Blade put his hands on her shoulders. Her rapid breathing and dilated pupils told him that she was truly scared.

"I'm sure he's just found a really good place to hide," he said calmly. "Let's look again and call out his name."

Josie wasted no time. She grabbed Blade's hand and pulled him up the stairs. "We'll start at the top and work down."

As she ran, Josie called for Archie to come out of his hiding place. She kept a tight hold of Blade's hand as if taking some strength from him. Although Blade was pretty certain that Archie was playing a clever game with them, even his heart rate began to increase when they were greeted with silence in every room. Their shouts attracted the attention of Detectives Pullman and Sykes, who came bounding up the stairs, weapons drawn, closely followed by a worried-looking Tim.

"We can't find Archie," Josie said breathlessly.

"He's gone." Blade felt her clammy hand squeeze his with ferocity. "Oh, no. Please, Lord, don't let him be hurt."

Blade raised an index finger to his lips. "Shh. I hear something."

They all fell silent, listening closely.

"There," said Blade as he heard a high-pitched giggling sound. "It seems to be coming from between the walls." He pointed to a bedroom that was unused and almost empty. "In here."

Letting go of Josie's hand, Blade rushed into the room and stood in the center for a moment. There were few places to hide. Just a bare bed and small closet were in the room, and both showed no trace of Archie. Yet the high-pitched giggling was clearly audible. Then he saw it—a small, well-concealed handle in the baseboard, low down and incredibly hard to see. There was obviously some storage space in the wall, designed to blend in almost seamlessly.

With a huge sigh of relief, Blade grabbed the handle and slid the panel across. There was Archie, curled up in a ball, a smile of pure joy on his face and peals of laughter coming from his mouth.

"You took forever to find me," he said, clambering out of the small space. "I'm good at this."

"Oh, Archie," Josie said, rushing forward and

scooping him up into her arms. "Why didn't you answer us when we called?"

Archie wrinkled his eyebrows as if this was a ridiculous question. "That would be cheating," he said earnestly. "You're supposed to find me all by yourself."

Blade watched the way that Josie gripped her son, clearly relieved to have found him safe and well. Archie, meanwhile, was oblivious to the distress he had caused and pushed away from his mother, saying, "Now it's your turn to hide, Mom."

"I think Mommy needs a rest now, sweetheart," Josie said, placing him on the floor. "I have to talk with Detective Sykes and look at some pictures, so why don't you play with your dad until I'm done?"

Blade looked down at his son's eager face. "I'd like to talk to Detective Sykes, too." He shot Tim a hopeful expression. "But I'm sure that Granddad would like to play."

Tim took Archie's hand. "I think that my old bones are too creaky for hide-and-seek, but I've been learning some new jokes. Do you want to hear them?"

Archie let out a dramatic groan. "I hope they're better than the last ones."

Tim laughed. "Much better." He took his grandson's hand and led him from the room.

Then Josie turned to Detectives Pullman and Sykes.

"Give me a few minutes, would you?" she asked, placing her hand over her heart to let them know that she was still recovering from the shock.

"Sure," Detective Sykes said. "Take your time."

When the detectives left the room, Josie's tears began to fall. Blade didn't need to ask why. She put one hand over her mouth to stifle the cries, and he heard her muffle the words, "I thought we'd lost him."

He took a step closer to her. In the next moment, Josie threw herself into his arms and clung to his shirt as if her life depended on it. She buried her face in his neck, and he felt her hot tears trickle onto his skin.

"It's okay," he said soothingly, snaking his arms around her waist and holding her tight. "He's safe. He'll always be safe with us."

Blade didn't know how long they stood there wrapped in each other's arms, but time seemed to stand still. It had been so long since he had held Josie this close, and the sensation was intoxicating. He remembered how fiercely he had loved her, how he had dreamed of a happy family life and how lonely he had been since abandoning her in Virginia. If only things had turned out differently. If only he hadn't lost his leg and destroyed his vision of the future.

The bond of a shared child drew him and Josie strongly together, but it wasn't enough to give them a future as a couple. He knew that. Nevertheless, as the minutes ticked by, he allowed himself to imagine what might have been.

Josie gave herself one last check in the mirror, smoothing back wispy strands of hair into her ponytail. She had slept badly, plagued by dark thoughts and scary dreams. She still hadn't fully recovered from the terror of failing to find Archie the previous day. Although he was out of her sight for only fifteen minutes, it had felt like hours. If Blade hadn't been there to give her extra strength and belief, it would have been unbearable. She was doing exactly what she promised herself she wouldn't: leaning on Blade emotionally. This wasn't a good situation, especially considering how often they clashed.

Josie was still smarting from the accusation that she was overprotective of her son. While she understood the need to allow a child some independence, in her opinion, Blade wanted to move too fast. Archie was still too young to go to the deep end of a swimming pool, even with an adult present. That wasn't being overprotective. That was simple common sense, wasn't it?

She heard Archie and Blade entering the bathroom, chatting contentedly together. To an outsider, the activities in this house would look like normal scenes of happy family life. But they were a facade. Soon Blade would return to North Carolina, and they would have to work out a co-parenting agreement.

Taking a deep breath and giving herself a last spritz of scent, she walked into the hallway and down the stairs. Today was likely to be the biggest day of the trial. Janice Weeks would be taking the stand. She, above all others, had the power to convince the jury of Norman's guilt. Miss Weeks was the only person who witnessed the alleged abduction, the only person to call the police. Her testimony could seal Norman's fate.

"Good morning, Josie," Detective Sykes said as she entered the kitchen. "You look ready to take on the day."

The detective was sitting at the kitchen table, poring over the mug shots that they had both already scrutinized the previous evening. Josie had looked at face after face of known criminals from the area, but none had matched the features of the man in the hat.

"I'm taking another look at these mug shots," Detective Sykes said, keeping her eyes focused on the pages. "Just in case we missed something." She swiveled the book toward Josie. "This guy looks like a possibility, don't you think?"

Josie sat down and looked hard at the bearded face in the picture. "No," she said. "The eyes are wrong. It's not him." She rubbed at her temples. "Maybe I don't recognize him at all. Maybe I'm imagining it."

The detective sighed and closed the book. "Don't worry about it for now. I've requested extra uniformed officers to escort you in and out of court today." She lowered her voice in case Archie might be lurking around the corner. "This man will not get another chance to take a shot at you, I promise."

Josie smiled weakly. Nobody in the police force could keep a promise like this.

Detective Sykes must have sensed Josie's apprehension. "Detective Pullman has already gone to the court to make sure that the extra security is in place," she said. "We're taking no chances." She smiled as they heard the front door open with a key and a voice call out a code word, letting them know he was a safe person. "Here he is now."

When Detective Pullman entered the kitchen, his expression was grave, and he took a seat at the table without a word.

"What's happened?" his colleague asked.

"Officers carried out a thorough search of the court building this morning," he replied. "I wanted to be absolutely sure that the place was clean."

Josie put her palms flat on the table. She guessed that something sinister had been uncovered.

"We found a device in the courtroom," Detective Pullman continued. "So we called in a team of experts to deal with it. The building has been evacuated, and the judge has halted the trial for today. Once the building has been thoroughly checked by the FBI, the trial will reconvene tomorrow."

Josie's stomach dropped. She didn't need to ask the question, but she did anyway.

"What did you find?"

"We believe it's a bomb. It was strapped to the underside of your seat in the courtroom."

SIX

"But...but how?" Josie stammered. "How could somebody get through security with a bomb?"

Detective Pullman shook his head. "We don't know. We're not yet certain that it *is* an explosive device. It has all the hallmarks of a homemade bomb, but it could be a hoax."

"What could be a hoax?" Blade asked, entering the kitchen, quickly followed by Archie.

Detective Sykes jumped up from her chair. "Hey, Archie," she said brightly. "I think it's time to go wake up your granddad. He said he'd like to make pancakes for you this morning." She took his hand. "I'll walk you upstairs."

Archie looked indignant at this comment. "I can walk upstairs by myself. I'm six years old now."

The detective smiled and led him toward the door. "Well, maybe *you* can walk *me* up the stairs," she said. "I'm a whole thirty years older than you, so I might need some help."

"Okay, sure," Archie said with a shrug of his slim shoulders. "I'm very good at helping old people."

Josie heard Detective Sykes laugh as they started up the stairs, and Blade waited until they were out of earshot before speaking.

"What happened?" he asked, placing a hand on Josie's shoulder. His touch was gentle.

"Officers found what looks like a bomb strapped beneath my chair," she replied. "The building is on lockdown." She put her head in her hands, leaning with her elbows on the table. "I could've been sitting in that chair in an hour." Her eyes flashed up at the clock on the wall, and she grabbed her cell. "I should call Norman."

"Don't worry," Detective Pullman said. "Officers are already on their way to his home to explain the situation."

Josie imagined Norman sitting in his house, alone and scared, all day. If that bomb had gone off today, he would have been in the blast zone, too. She was fortunate to be surrounded by her family and two Wichita detectives giving her comfort and reassurance. Norman had no company inside his home, and his loneliness was apparent every time she paid a visit. He just wanted the trial to be over, but it had stalled as soon as it had begun. She knew that this delay would hit him hard.

"I'd like to go and see Norman today," she said. "He'll be running low on groceries, so I should take him some supplies."

Detective Pullman looked apprehensive. "In light of the situation, I think it would be better to stay at the safe house today."

Josie wouldn't accept this. "I'm an attorney, and Norman is my client. It's important that I make sure he knows exactly what's going on and is advised accordingly." She lifted her chin. "I will not become a prisoner in this house because of a coward who hides behind bombs and guns."

She saw Blade smile widely. "Good for you. I'll come along, too."

"I figured you would."

Their eyes lingered on each other just a little too long, and Josie felt a spark of old attraction catch. She and Blade used to have no secrets and were as close as two people could possibly be. She saw flashes of the man he used to be, yet he was very different now. Even though he seemed to have accepted the loss of his leg with grace and humility, he was touchy whenever she asked questions or offered assistance. She had reached a point of exasperation. Blade had run ten miles every evening since his arrival in Sedgwick, but he hadn't once discussed the Invictus Games in depth with her. It was as though he didn't want to let her into that part of his life. Maybe it was a deliberate ploy on his part. After all, they disagreed on so many things already. It made sense to keep their relationship simple.

"We can't afford to be too complacent," Detective Pullman said. "Before you go anywhere, our SUV must be thoroughly checked for devices." He rose from his chair. "I'll go check on it right now."

The detective exited the kitchen via the door that led into the garage, and Josie was suddenly aware of the absolute silence between her and Blade, broken only by the tick of the clock on the wall. She decided to bite the bullet and try to build a bridge between them.

"Blade," she said. "Can I ask you something?"

He looked apprehensive. "Sure."

"How does it feel to have lost a limb?"

He seemed taken aback at the bluntness of the question, but Josie liked to straight-talk. It was part of her job, a long-established habit that she couldn't break.

"I'm sorry," she said. "I don't mean to pry. The conversation we had about Archie yesterday made me realize that we hardly know each other anymore."

When Blade didn't respond, she started to rise from her chair. "Forget I said anything."

"It's okay," he said. "I want you to feel comfortable enough to ask me anything." He laughed.

"But after what happened at the courthouse this morning, I figured you wanted to ask me something about bombs."

She sat back down. "I can't change my situation, so I don't see any point in scaring myself with details about the damage bombs can inflict." She glanced down at his leg. "You don't talk about yourself or the past. It's pretty obvious that we're very different people, with totally different parenting styles." She thought of Archie struggling to swim in a pool, his toes unable to reach the bottom, and she shuddered. "So I figured I should get to know the person you are now a little better."

"Losing a limb is different for everyone," he said. "But for me, it's been both the best and worst experience of my life." He looked out the window, staring into the distance. "Right after the amputation, the residual limb hurt like crazy, and I was angry all the time." He stole a glance at her face. "But you know that already, because you were there."

She nodded. "I was wondering how it feels now. Does it still hurt?"

He visibly relaxed. "The leg gets sore every now and again, but it's not too bad. What really bothers me is when I get phantom limb pain. An amputee can often feel sensations in a limb that's no longer there, and occasionally I get itches or aches where my leg used to be. It sounds crazy, but it happens."

"I watched you run down the street last night," she said. "You move so fast. How does it feel to run on a blade?"

His voice took on a faraway tone. "Imagine being locked in a tiny prison for five years and then having the door opened." He took a slow, deep breath. "It feels like freedom. When I run, I'm whole again."

She visualized him jogging, lithe and fluid. His movements were so elegant and graceful, and she found herself captivated when she caught sight of him running as she stood at her bedroom window.

"You make it look so easy," she said.

"It took a lot of practice to get my balance and coordination right. I crashed to the ground more times than I care to admit, but once I mastered the technique, it was surprisingly simple." He fell silent for a moment. "People look at me differently when I run. They can see I'm an athlete, and they don't pity me."

She was surprised. "Does anybody pity you?"

"Oh, sure they do," he replied. "There are some people in my hometown who treat me like an invalid. My elderly neighbor once offered to walk me across the street, and the bag boys at the grocery store always ask if I need help to my car." He shrugged. "I can't change how other people see me, and I know they're acting out of kindness, but it's infuriating sometimes."

Something in his voice concerned her. "Do you think *I* pity you?" she asked.

He looked her straight in the eye. "I don't know. *Do* you?"

"Absolutely not."

"You sure about that?"

She cocked her head to the side, uncertain of what he was getting at. "Yes."

"You've offered to help me out of a chair, carry my bags and walk me upstairs. You've also told me how important it is to protect my good leg," he said, counting the incidents off on his fingers. "That sure feels like pity to me."

"That's different," Josie protested. "I didn't do those things because I pity you. I just wanted to support you."

"But you don't understand how it makes me feel, Josie," Blade said, leaning in close. "I get why you want to help me, but it just reinforces the idea that I'm weaker than others. Even though most people assume they don't judge me, there are times when everybody treats me differently, including you. I know that I'm strong and capable, but I have a hard time convincing others of the same thing."

Josie's face burned with indignation. Was she

really as inconsiderate as he was alleging? Or was Blade being hypersensitive? After all, offering to help somebody out of a chair was pretty inoffensive, wasn't it?

"So when people ask me how it feels to lose a limb," Blade said, rising and walking to the coffeepot, "it's an uncomfortable question to answer, because sometimes I have to call them out on their prejudices."

"I think that's a little unfair, Blade. I don't see you as disabled."

Blade filled his mug. "Okay."

The way he said this one word infuriated her, as if he was patronizing her.

"This is ridiculous," she said. "I've allowed you to act as my bodyguard. I see you as strong and capable."

"Josie," Blade said, leaning against the counter, arms folded. "I know you're a good person and you mean well, but you have to trust me on this. You definitely don't treat me the same way you treat everybody else. I've battled against prejudice for seven years, and I can spot it a mile off."

Josie's face burned hotter, and a defensive streak rushed through her. Blade was calling her out as narrow-minded, and he was wrong.

"I'm sorry if I hurt your feelings by offering assistance when I thought you needed it," she said, keeping her voice flat and smooth as if she were in court. "I'll try to change if it helps."

"It would."

"Okay," she said with a vigorous nod. She was bristling with annoyance. "I'm glad we got that cleared up."

At that moment, Detective Pullman reentered the kitchen, rubbing his hands on an oily rag. Josie was so grateful for the distraction, preventing the need to continue her awkward and strained conversation with Blade.

"We're all clear. I went over that car with a fine-tooth comb," the detective said, sitting at the table. "I also received confirmation from the bomb squad that the device beneath your chair was a fake. Its purpose was to create fear rather than to harm you. This guy is toying with us."

"Well, he won't stop me from getting on with things today," Josie said, rising to busy herself, opening cupboards to pull out boxes and cans that she could take to Norman's house. "I'd like to leave soon."

She felt Blade's hand on her back and straightened up.

"Thanks for the chat," he said. "It helped a lot."

"Great," she said tersely, twisting her body away from his. "I'm glad."

She continued to rifle through the cupboards,

trying to avoid his gaze. Their discussion might have helped Blade, but it had done no such thing for her. If anything, the yawning abyss that existed between them had grown even wider. She was already losing the affections of her son to his rough-and-tumble father, and now that same man was accusing her of being insensitive about his disability.

With the continual threats and danger already weighing heavily on her shoulders, Josie didn't know if she had the strength to accept this new burden.

She wondered if she was about to reach her breaking point.

Blade narrowed his eyes in the dark, musty living room of Norman Francis. With the drapes closed, the only light entering the room was from a bulb overhead. The dinginess was depressing, and he found himself full of sympathy for this reclusive man who was confined to his home twenty-four hours a day. At least the room was warm, heated by an open fire in the hearth.

"I brought you some groceries," Josie said, placing a bag on the floor between two threadbare sofas. "It's not much, but it'll see you through the week."

"Thank you," Norman said, bending down to take the bag in his left hand.

Josie sprang forward. "Let me help you with that," she said. Then she stood up straight, glancing sideways at Blade. "Sorry—I'm sure you've got it covered."

"You look tired, Josie," Norman said. "Are you okay?"

Josie waved the question away with a flick of her wrist. "I'm just fine. I'm not sleeping well, but that's understandable, right? I'm sure things will improve as I settle into the trial."

"Why don't you take a seat and relax," Norman said, heading for the kitchen with the groceries. "I'll make some hot, sweet tea. I think it's just what we all need after the shock of this morning's bomb scare."

Blade sank into a chair next to a table on which stood a number of exquisitely carved wooden figurines. He noticed Josie choose the chair that was the farthest possible distance from his. She looked uncomfortable in his presence, and he guessed that their earlier discussion was the cause. But he had only spoken the words that needed to be said. If he and Josie were to have any kind of civil relationship, he had to be straight with her.

"This is really beautiful," he said, picking up a figurine and focusing his attention on it. It was a horse with a rider on top, all carved from one single piece of wood. "Look at the detail. It's incredible."

"Norman usually sells them at craft fairs and shows," Josie said. "But he hasn't been able to attend them since being under house arrest, so he lives on almost nothing."

Blade cast his eyes around the room. "He definitely doesn't seem like a man with a lot of money to splash around." His gaze came to rest on an open Bible on a fireside table. "But I guess he manages just fine."

He watched Josie hook her hair behind her ears self-consciously. The awkwardness between them seemed to have grown to huge proportions. Not only had they clashed on the best way to parent their child, but also he had now challenged the way she treated his disability. It was hard to believe that they had once loved each other deeply. His physical attraction to her was still strong, but it would never be enough to sustain a happy relationship. He knew that.

"It's nice to have company," Norman said, entering the room, balancing a tray on one hand. Blade noticed Josie automatically shift in her chair as if wanting to take the tray from Norman's grasp, but she stopped herself and watched him slide it onto the coffee table.

"Could one of you take a cup to the detective

sitting in the car outside?" he asked. "Are you sure she doesn't want to come in?"

"She says she's happier in the car with her travel mug of coffee," Josie said. "There are some workmen digging up the street, and there's a lot of activity making her uneasy."

Norman's eyes flicked nervously to the window. "I see. I try not to take much notice of what goes on outside."

"How are you holding up, Norm?" Josie asked. "I keep telling you that you look too thin. Why don't you sit down?"

Norman remained standing, his anxiety evident in his posture. "I haven't been eating much lately. I don't do enough activity to work up an appetite. I mostly spend my days carving and watching TV." He looked at the drape-covered window, which overlooked his backyard. "My fence blew down last week, so I had to go outside and secure it, but Janice saw me and yelled something. I didn't catch the words, but she was mad, so I came back inside and left the fence on the lawn."

Josie sighed. "Don't let her bully you, Norman. She's not supposed to have any contact with you until the trial is over. We could file a complaint."

"No, don't do that," Norman said, a panicked

look falling across his face. "It'll probably just make her worse. She seems to really hate me."

Josie leaned forward in her chair. "I know we've discussed this a thousand times before, but have you thought of any reason why Janice would lie about seeing you lead Lisa by the hand into your home?"

Norman shook his head while bending to pour three cups of tea. "I've been over it time and time again in my head, and I just can't come up with an answer. I can only assume that she's mistaken. Even Janice wouldn't lie about something so terrible."

Josie smiled. "That's very generous of you, Norman, but the only conclusion I can come to regarding Janice's witness statement is that she's deliberately lying. She never saw you take Lisa inside your home because it simply didn't happen."

Blade took the cup that Norman offered him. "Have you always had a difficult relationship with your neighbor, Norman?"

"I'm afraid so," the older man said, taking a seat next to Blade. "Her dogs bark all through the night, keeping me awake. I asked her to do something about it a few times, and she took offense. Her yard is real small, so I offered mine as a place where she could exercise the dogs, but she acted like she didn't want to come anywhere near my house. She called me 'creepy.'"

Josie let out a short, exasperated puff of breath as if she'd grown incensed by this type of bullying behavior.

Norman took a sip of tea. "I grew up being called names like 'creepy' and 'weird' by kids in school, so I'm kinda used to it, although it never stops hurting." He turned to Blade. "I have a mild form of cerebral palsy, which you can probably see from my movements. When I was in fifth grade, I decided I'd try to hide my disability by wearing clothes that cover most of my body." He gave a strangled laugh. "But the large sweaters and pants I wore just gave people something else to laugh at."

"Does Janice know that you were born with cerebral palsy?" Blade asked.

"No," Norman said firmly. "None of my neighbors are aware of my condition, and I don't want them to know. I don't want their pity."

Blade couldn't help his eyes flicking to Josie. She kept her gaze downcast, and her color reddened. She said nothing.

"Don't you think it would help your relationship with your neighbors if you were open and honest with them?" Blade asked. "People might surprise you by being very understanding."

"I've been trying to hide my cerebral palsy

for most of my life," Norman replied. "I don't expect you know how that feels, but it's not an easy habit to break."

"Actually," Blade said, pulling up the leg of his jeans, "I understand perfectly. I lost my lower leg seven years ago, and I've been attempting to walk normally ever since. When you have a disability, sometimes all you want to do is look like a regular Joe."

Norman stared openmouthed at the prosthetic leg for a few seconds. "Well, I'd never have guessed," he said finally. "You do a pretty good job of passing for able-bodied."

Blade smiled knowingly. "When I got my first prosthesis, all I wanted to do was pass as able-bodied. I wore long pants all the time, even in one-hundred-degree heat. I didn't want anybody to see that I was disabled, so I practiced walking normally for hours and hours until my limb bled. I just didn't want to be different."

Norman picked up one of his carved figurines and caressed it in his hands. "You're fortunate that you're able to compensate for your disability so well. Mine is much more noticeable." He held the figurine in midair and it jerked slightly. "As you can see, I have very poor coordination in the muscles of my right arm and right leg. Even though my condition is mild compared to others', it's almost impossible for me to look like a regular person."

"Then why try?" Blade asked. "I stopped trying years ago. These days I wear shorts, I go swimming and I never hide my prosthesis or my residual limb. Do people stare? Yes, of course they do, but I don't care. I am who I am." He noticed Josie concentrating on his face, listening closely. "It's liberating to face the world without a mask."

Norman shook his head. "You're a much younger and braver man than I am, Mr. Harding. I'm almost seventy years old. I couldn't face the world without my overcoat."

Josie cleared her throat. "Norman won't even let me refer to his condition in the trial. I think it's highly relevant and will allow the jury to understand his character more fully."

"I already told you, Josie," Norman said, his voice unwavering. "I don't want anybody's pity."

"But I wish you'd at least consider it," she said. "The jury sees you sitting in the courtroom swamped by a huge coat, and they assume you have something to hide. They won't get a chance to see the real you."

"That suits me just fine," he said. "I'd rather they didn't see the real me. If people knew about my cerebral palsy, they'd probably treat me even worse than they do now. They'd either pity me or mock me, and I'm not sure which one is worse."

"Think about the alternative," Blade said. "Which is them seeing you as a child abuser."

"I know it may seem strange to you, but I'd rather suffer the consequences than be judged as weak and pitiful."

Blade felt a kinship with Norman. "The opinions of others don't matter. By trying to hide yourself away, you're giving them too much power over your happiness. Trust me, I know this. I hid away for too long." His eyes flicked over to the Bible and saw the pages open to the book of Job. "Job was afraid of the opinions of others, too. He said, 'I feared the great multitude. And the contempt of families terrified me. And I kept silent and stayed indoors.' But like you, Job had done nothing wrong and had no reason to be ashamed."

A tremor gripped Norman's hand, and he held both palms tightly together as if in prayer. He remained silent for some time, head bowed.

"You know your Bible well," he said, looking up. "The book of Job is one of my favorites." He smiled, revealing the fact that a couple of teeth were missing. "And I guess that this particular verse would seem to sum up my situation pretty well." He raised his eyebrows as if seeing the parallel for the first time. "I *do* keep silent and stay indoors most of the time." He pointed to the electronic tag secured around his leg. "Even before I had this ankle bracelet."

"So why not throw off the shackles and allow others to see your true self?" Blade asked. "Why don't you allow Josie to reveal your condition to the jury?"

Norman was unmoved. "I appreciate what you're trying to do, but I'm not prepared to do that. You're asking too much of me."

Blade had expected this. The first time he had worn shorts with his prosthesis, he had been sick with nerves, worried about the stares of others.

"Okay," Blade said. "But promise me that you'll at least pray about it."

Norman's eyes traveled to the well-worn Bible on the table, and he seemed deep in thought before slowly nodding. "I'll do that."

Finally Blade was making progress, so he pushed a little further. "And you'll consider changing your mind?"

"I said I'll pray about it," Norman repeated. "God will lead me from there." He picked up his tea. "But can we please change the subject now?" He looked directly at Josie. "I carved a bird for Archie. It's a scale model of a parakeet." He reached beneath the couch and pulled out a box full of Bubble Wrap. "Now, where did I put it?" He rummaged around inside. "I copied it from a book."

As Norman searched for the carving, Blade tried to catch Josie's eye, but she avoided his gaze, staring into the fire, lost in thought. He wondered what was going through her mind. Was she still angry with him regarding his earlier accusations? The look on her face told him nothing.

He wasn't sure that it mattered, anyway. He hadn't yet found a way to navigate the gulf between them. And he didn't know if he ever would.

Josie waved to Norman as he stood at the window, watching his visitors get into their SUV. She knew that her visits buoyed Norman, and she was glad to be able to help, but this particular visit had affected her profoundly. Norman's experience of living with a disability seemed to echo Blade's, and it forced her to reevaluate whether Blade had been correct to call her out on her failings. While in Norman's home, she had wanted to help him with the groceries, to take the tray of tea from his hand and to ensure that he didn't strain himself. It was exactly how she treated Blade. And she had begun to see things through his eyes.

"Thanks for what you did back there," she said

to Blade. "I've never gotten that far in persuading Norman to allow the jury to know about his condition. I've been working on him for over a year, but it took you only ten minutes to get him to open up a little."

"I think he just needed to hear that he's not the only one to struggle with an impairment," Blade said. "He's tried to cope on his own for so long, he's forgotten how many other disabled people are out there, living regular lives."

She fell silent, realizing that Blade and Norman's shared experience of disability gave them common ground—one she couldn't be part of. And one she simply didn't understand, no matter how hard she tried.

"I'm sorry," she said.

"About what?"

"About my behavior toward you." Josie was too embarrassed to look at him, so she focused on Norman standing at the window, pulling the drape aside, peering both ways down the street. "I was angry when you challenged me about treating you differently. I just didn't see it. I thought you were being overly sensitive."

She glanced up to see Blade smile as Detective Sykes pulled slowly away from the curbside and onto the street. Josie gave Norman one last wave, feeling a little tug on her heart to see his downcast expression as he let the drape fall over the window once again.

"And what changed your mind?" Blade asked.

She finally turned to face him, seeing him give her his full attention, and she felt the pressure of choosing the right words to convey her sincerity.

"No matter how hard I try to imagine it, I'll never know how you or Norman feels. I'll never know the hurt caused by a throwaway comment or the humiliation of being helped across the street. I can never know these things because I'm not part of your world, and I can't walk in your shoes. Seeing you connect with Norman so easily made me realize how little I truly comprehend." She played with a strand of hair, unused to admitting a personal failing. "I guess that being an attorney has made me arrogant. I assume that I can get inside everybody's head." She laughed nervously. "But I can't get inside yours."

Blade said nothing, and she dug her fingernails into the palms of her hands, waiting for confirmation that her apology had been accepted.

Finally the silence was too much. "Please say something, Blade."

The next words from his mouth were not ones she had been expecting.

"Watch out!" he yelled to Detective Sykes as the car neared an intersection. "Stop!"

But the detective didn't react quickly enough to the danger that Blade had seen. Josie had no idea what was happening, but she heard the tires blow beneath the car with a series of huge bangs, and she put her hands over her ears in shock. The SUV began to veer from side to side as their driver struggled to control their path. The vehicle plowed into a line of traffic cones that had cordoned off a hole in the ground, where workmen were laying cables.

Josie felt Blade pull her close and hold her tight as the men scattered in all directions, and the car plunged headlong into the ditch with a sickening crunch.

SEVEN

Josie felt the weight of her body being supported partially by the seat belt and partially by Blade. The car was sitting almost upright in the hole, its back wheels off the ground. Detective Sykes seemed to be unconscious, limp and facedown in the inflated air bag.

"Detective!" Josie shouted. "Are you okay?"

No answer.

Josie looked to Blade, panicked. "What do we do?"

Blade maneuvered his body around before unclipping his belt and positioning himself, back-to-back, against the driver's seat.

"We need to get to safety," he said. "I saw a spike strip slide across the road, and whoever is responsible will be waiting to attack again."

There was a loud knocking at the back window and Josie let out a small scream of shock. It was one of the workmen, wearing a yellow hard hat.

"Are you people all right?" he yelled. "Should I call an ambulance?"

Blade pulled the handle of the door and tried to open it, but it was jammed against the side of the hole where they were wedged. He tried the window, but with the engine off, the electrical system wasn't functioning.

"Yes, call 911!" Blade yelled back. "But can you get us out first?"

The workman held up a hammer, and Blade nodded enthusiastically. He then scooted over to Josie and cradled her head in his arms as the window was smashed with a bang. The man tapped at the glass around the edges, making a safe space through which they could crawl out onto the street.

He leaned into the car and reached out his fingers. "Here. Take my hand."

Just as she stretched her arm toward him, Blade pulled her back. "I should go first. We don't know who's out there." He glanced at Detective Sykes, who remained still and impassive. "I don't think we should move her. We don't know what injuries she has. I'll get outside and stand guard until the police arrive."

"But, Blade, you shouldn't risk…" she started to protest before remembering her apology of only seconds ago. She was backsliding already. "Just stay safe out there."

He touched her cheek gently. "I will."

In the next moment, she saw Blade's legs sail through the window as he was pulled by the man in the hard hat. Once he had planted both feet on the ground, she unclipped her belt and fell forward, supporting herself on the front seats, before twisting into the gap between the driver's and passenger seats. Then she took a closer look at Detective Sykes, noticing a gash above her right eye. When Josie softly laid a hand on the detective's back, the older woman groaned and flicked her eyes open.

"Don't worry," Josie whispered. "It's all under control."

When the detective once again faded into unconsciousness, Josie pressed her hands together and closed her eyes tight. There were so many people who needed the Lord's protection at that moment, and Josie had faith that He would take care of them all.

It was only when the sound of gunshots rocked the air that she began to have doubts.

Blade threw himself to the ground behind a car parked at the curb and pulled his gun from its holster. Six of the workmen who had been laying cables in the road ran for their lives, disappearing behind the nearest house. Yet Blade was sure there had been seven workmen. Where was the missing man? He lifted his head and saw one of the workers cowering beneath a tree, hugging it tightly as if his life depended on it. As the shooting ceased, Blade stood up, desperately searching for the attacker, but a volley of bullets forced him to the ground again. He was only about six feet from the stranded SUV, which was protruding from the large hole like a beached whale, awkward and bulky, totally defenseless.

The bullets began to fly once more, unrelenting, coming thick and fast. Blade heard the unmistakable pop of holes opening up in metal, and he was flooded with dread. He was supposed to be protecting Josie. He had promised to act as her bodyguard, yet he was failing. He knew the attacker must be nearby, but he had no idea where.

"Come on, Blade," he said to himself. "Think."

That was when his mind returned to the cowering workman under the tree. The bullets seemed to be coming from his direction. Blade dragged himself along the asphalt to get a better vantage point beneath the car that was shielding him. He could see a man in a yellow hard hat holding a gun. This was the shooter, masquerading as a frightened roadside worker.

Blade rolled farther under the car and started firing off rounds in response. The man fell backward, obviously surprised by the sudden show of defense. But he recovered quickly and positioned himself behind the tree to begin a renewed assault. His bullets pounded the asphalt, kicking up grit and dirt, but Blade didn't let the attack drive him back. He maintained his position, feeling as though he had been transported back in time to his SEAL days, back to a time when he would gladly die for the man by his side. That was exactly how he felt about Josie at that moment. She was the mother of his child, and her life must be protected at all costs.

When his weapon was empty, he frantically pulled at his jacket pocket, trying to find his replacement magazine. It wasn't there. In the ensuing silence, the shooter took his chance, jumping out from behind the tree and rushing toward Blade, gun at his side. Blade saw a pair of black boots coming ever closer, realizing that he was seconds away from a speeding bullet. He rolled away, patting all his pockets in a desperate search for more ammunition. But he found none. His time was up.

When shots rang out, loud and clear, Blade waited for the stinging pain of a bullet in his flesh. Yet he felt nothing. It was then that he realized the gunshots were coming from inside the SUV. The black boots that had been advancing on him now turned and hurried away, using parked vehicles as shields until he could vault a fence and vanish from sight. Blade scrambled from his horizontal position and bounced to his feet, instinctively raising his weapon even though it was unloaded.

He saw Josie, her body leaning through the window of the SUV, perfectly poised with a gun in her hand. The look on her face was one of pure determination, and when she saw him, her features relaxed into a smile.

"You okay?" she called out.

"Yeah," he shouted. "Thanks for having my back." He watched her maintain her strong pose, not lowering her weapon, clearly not taking any chances. "I didn't know you had a gun."

She finally brought the weapon to her side when two police cars appeared at the end of the street, sirens blaring. "Public defenders have to be prepared for anything," she said. "I don't like to pull my gun, but it's always there if I need it." She held up a black rectangular device. It was the replacement magazine for his gun. "And when I saw this on the floor of the car, I figured you might be in trouble."

He smiled at her, full of admiration for her clear thinking and bravery. She had almost certainly saved his life. Just a few hours ago, they were fighting like cats and dogs, yet now they were successfully working together to overcome the threats bearing down on them. Had they turned a corner at last? Could they now move forward as a more unified force and put their bickering behind them?

Even as these thoughts entered his head, he dismissed them. One experience of cooperation didn't overcome their differences. It was wishful thinking on his part. There were still plenty of stormy clouds ahead. He was sure of it.

Josie hung up the phone after speaking with Norman for over an hour. At the scene of the attack, she and Blade had seen Detective Sykes safely into an ambulance. Then they had been driven home by a police officer in an unmarked car, who carefully avoided being followed by taking a long and convoluted route home. But she didn't mind. Her biggest fear right now was her attacker discovering their safe house. She had begun to wonder whether she had made the right decision in keeping Archie with her. Would her aunt Susan's house in Nebraska be a safer option after all? She knew Blade would disagree, and she didn't want to clash with him, but their situation was now too dangerous to ignore. She would have to raise the issue again.

She walked into the living room and sat on the couch opposite Blade and Archie. Archie was doodling on a piece of paper with a pencil, making big sweeping lines, interspersed with words like *cool* and *awesome*.

"What you drawing there, honey?" Josie asked, turning her head to see the image the right way up.

Archie swiveled the sketch pad around. "I'm designing some flying shoes," he said proudly. He pointed to the soles, where crude stink lines had been drawn. "They get their power from manure."

Josie laughed. It felt strange to find amusement on a day that had been fraught with danger, but she welcomed it.

"Manure?" she asked. "That's a pretty odd choice of fuel."

Archie nodded enthusiastically. "I know, but I heard that cows pass a lot of wind, so I figured that their poop is full of gas." He turned the paper back around to continue sketching. "I think it's called methane."

Blade patted his son on the back, chuckling. "That's right, son," he said. "But there might be a few flaws in your idea. I'll help you work on them later." He looked at Josie, clearly sensing her desire to talk. "Why don't you go show your invention to Granddad? He's in the kitchen."

Archie hopped off the couch and padded across the carpet in his socks. "Okay."

Once he was in the other room, Blade turned to Josie, waiting for her to speak first.

"Norman is pretty shaken up by what's happened," she said. "He feels responsible for being the bait in the attack. This guy would've known I'd be likely to visit Norman today, so he lay in wait until I showed up. The police decided to post a twenty-four-hour guard outside Norman's home, just to be on the safe side."

Blade knit his fingers together and brought them up to his face, using them like a shelf on which to rest his chin. "Something just doesn't add up here," he said. "Whoever wants to punish you for representing Norman doesn't seem interested in taking vengeance on Norman himself. This guy knows where your client lives, but he's never made a move to attack him directly. Doesn't that strike you as odd?"

This had also been on Josie's mind. "I've been thinking the exact same thing."

"I have a theory," said Blade. "Could your attacker be using the trial as a smoke screen?" He shifted on the couch, leaning toward her. "Think about it. There's a whole heap of negative publicity and angry demonstrations about taxpayer money being used to assist a child abductor who is supposed to have thousands of dollars stashed away. It's the perfect cover for someone who holds a grudge against you. It totally throws the police off the scent."

This made sense to Josie. "You could be right." She closed her eyes, trying to conjure up the image of her attacker's face. "I assumed that I recognized the man in the baseball hat from the area, but he could be anybody from my past. I've defended a lot of nasty characters over the years. Any one of those people could be using Norman's trial as an opportunity to punish me for failing to secure a not-guilty verdict."

"Do you remember anyone ever threatening you after they were found guilty?" Blade asked.

She couldn't stop a shiver snaking down her spine. "Quite a few times, actually. I've had clients threaten to destroy my car or burn down my home." She shrugged her shoulders, trying to shake off the fear that came with the territory of her job. "But the worst threats came from a man who said he would enjoy toying with me and watching me die when he got out of jail. I got the sense that he really meant it."

This piqued Blade's interest. "Who was that? Tell me about him."

Josie cast her mind back. "I represented a guy named Orlando Cardwell three years ago. He was a high-profile investment fund manager, and he had a huge portfolio of wealthy clients across Kansas." She smiled wryly, remembering the arrogance of the man, his unshakable belief in his own importance. "He was well-known for his glamorous parties and charity functions. But it turned out that he was using his clients' money to finance his own business ventures and personal expenses. In total, he stole eleven and a half million dollars."

Blade gave a low whistle through his teeth. "Wow. His parties must have been expensive."

"He frittered away millions on stocks and shares in companies that subsequently collapsed, and none of his business projects were a success. By the time he was caught he was penniless, living on credit cards and bank loans. It was humiliating for him to have to resort to using a public defender, but he had no choice. All his assets were seized."

"And you lost the case?"

Josie threw her hands in the air. "Of course I did. The case against him was the tightest I've ever known. I strongly advised him to accept a plea bargain, but he was so egotistical, he never dreamed that the jury would see through his lies. It was no surprise that he blamed me for our disastrous defense. He took no responsibility for his own actions at all."

"The guy attacking you is clinical, ruthless and wants you dead," Blade said. "And Mr.

Cardwell sounds like he would certainly fit the profile."

Josie folded her arms. This was where Blade's theory came unglued. "Orlando Cardwell is serving thirty-five years in the Lansing Correctional Facility."

Blade obviously didn't see this as a barrier. "If he wanted to get to you, he could use the services of others."

This didn't seem likely to Josie. "But he's been in jail for two years already, and he's reportedly been a model prisoner. He even offers the other inmates financial advice, crazy as it sounds."

Blade took a deep breath and rubbed a hand down his stubbly face. "It makes sense to check him out. I'll ask Detective Pullman to send someone to interview him at Leavenworth."

Josie sighed. She thought that Blade was grasping at straws. It was like looking for a needle in a haystack.

He seemed to know how she was feeling. "It's a process of elimination," he said. "So let's come up with a list of suspects and check them out one by one."

She tried to rally herself. This was the kind of process she had undertaken hundreds of times before, methodically and painstakingly crafting the best defense cases she could build by checking off those with a motive to commit a crime.

But her mind and spirit were weak, worn down by the stress of the attacks.

"Sure," she said with a false smile. "It won't hurt to try."

He leaned across the table and picked up a pen and sheet of paper. "Okay. Start from the beginning of your career and name as many people as you can think of who might be crazy enough to want you dead."

She took a deep breath. This was hard. She didn't particularly want to be reminded of how wicked and malicious some of her clients had been. She'd defended all kinds of evil people over the years, constantly reminding herself that every citizen was entitled to representation.

As she trawled her memory to come up with the names of all her disgruntled clients, her heart sank further and further in her chest. The list of possibilities grew until they were faced with eight names—eight men who had been convicted of crimes ranging from domestic violence to murder. And all of them blamed their defense counsel for their incarceration.

"I'll see what I can find out about these criminals," Blade said, folding the paper and putting it in the pocket of his shirt. "If the local police won't help, I have a contact in the FBI who can probably pull some records."

"Thank you, Blade," she said a little awkwardly. "I appreciate you helping me out like this."

"You're welcome," he said with a smile. "I'm glad to do it."

She glanced toward the kitchen doorway. Now seemed like a good a time as any to raise her concerns about Archie. "In light of what happened today, I've been reconsidering Archie's living arrangements."

She saw Blade tense up.

"I'm so worried," she continued. "What if this guy manages to find us here? I can't stop thinking about it."

"Archie is perfectly safe," Blade said. "The house is secure with round-the-clock protection, and most importantly, he's happy. Why fix something that isn't broken?"

Josie twisted an earring. She had guessed that this would be Blade's response. After all, he was more willing to take risks with Archie's personal safety than she was.

"Why wait for something to break before fixing it?" she asked, looking him dead in the eye. The acid taste of fear traveled up her throat as she imagined a gun being pointed at the beautiful blond curls of her sweet child. "If it were up to you, I'm sure Archie would be swinging from the rafters, playing with a chain saw." It was a wild analogy, but it summed up how she felt.

Blade raised his eyebrows in surprise. "Now, hold on a minute. I know we might have different ideas about what's best for Archie, but I'd never let him do anything truly dangerous."

Josie gritted her teeth, trying not to let her words come flying out before considering them.

"I just don't think you fully comprehend what's at stake here," she said quietly. "You're an ex-SEAL. Staring bad guys in the face is normal to you, but Archie's a little kid. He's already witnessed a shoot-out on the street and had a brick thrown through his bedroom window, and who knows what effect that incident might have had on his emotional well-being."

Blade smiled as if she'd said something ridiculous.

"Archie's emotional well-being is just fine," he said calmly. "He's not worried about the bad guys. He's worried about how to make flying shoes from cow manure. You can see how happy and content he is. Kids are resilient."

Josie stood and paced the room, feeling her anxiety levels rise. This conversation wasn't going as well as she'd hoped.

"I know you think I'm overprotective," she said defensively. "But I happen to think that you're a little too relaxed about Archie's safety. He's going to stay with my aunt Susan, and that's final."

Blade stood to face her. "So my opposition to this plan is irrelevant, huh?"

"Yes," she said, raising her voice and crossing her arms. "I'm overruling you."

He shook his head and looked at the floor, hooking his thumbs through his belt loops. "You're overruling me? This isn't a court of law, Josie. This is a family discussion."

"How can this be a family discussion?" she asked incredulously. "We're not a real family. We just happen to share a child together. I've been a mother for six years, and you've been a father for five days. I know what's best for Archie."

Blade's face crumpled, but he regained composure quickly. "Don't you trust me to keep our boy safe?" he said, raising his voice. "Is that what all this is about?"

Hot, stinging tears pricked at Josie's eyelids. She didn't want to make Blade feel inadequate, but their son's life might depend on her ability to make decent and rational choices.

"No!" she shouted. "I don't trust you to keep Archie safe."

There. She had finally said it.

Her father poked his head out of the kitchen. "Everything okay out here?"

"Sorry, Dad," Josie said, wiping a tear quickly

away from her cheek. "Our discussion got a little heated."

Tim looked between her and Blade with concern. "Why not take a time-out? Dinner will be ready soon."

"I'll go get freshened up," Josie said, turning and walking from the room, glad to have an opportunity to make her escape. Blade sometimes made her feel stifled, like she couldn't breathe. Her color had risen and her pulse had quickened, almost the same symptoms as being in love, yet without any of the benefits.

She heard Blade call after her as she ran upstairs. "Josie, can we talk later?"

She didn't reply. Their relationship had become so complicated. One minute they were working together in perfect harmony, yet in the next they were fighting again. It was exhausting.

But where Archie was concerned, she had no intention of backing down.

Blade ran harder and faster than he ever had before, pumping his arms rhythmically in time with his legs. The sweat ran through his hair and down his back, and he enjoyed feeling the stress of the day flow from his body. He was angry, frustrated, exasperated and just about ready to throw in the towel. He had just endured an uncomfortable and strained family dinner, with

Archie clearly picking up on the tension between his parents. It wasn't good for a child to be caught in the middle of a disagreement, and they would have to find a way of dealing amicably with their differences of opinion.

Blade knew it would be a difficult process of working himself into Josie's life, and he'd been prepared for some hiccups along the way, but he wondered if the bumps in the road would ever end. Josie's earlier apology had been encouraging, giving him hope that she might be prepared to cooperate a little more on parenting. But she had quickly reverted to her old self by placing her views above his. It hurt him deeply to know that she didn't want to entrust the care of Archie to him. Blade had gotten that message loud and clear. Josie believed herself to be the better parent, and he was consigned to the margins. He knew many divorced dads who had to be content with taking their kids on the occasional day trip, rarely involved in the major decisions of their children's lives. It was unfair to both the fathers and children.

Blade pushed himself to run even faster. If Josie expected him to be a father in name only, then she was wrong. He had just as much right to be involved in parenting decisions as she did. But he would have to take a soft and gentle approach if he was to make any headway. Being at odds with a successful and driven defense attorney was not something he wanted to continue.

There was no other way to fight this particular battle than with humility. Just like Job, Blade would have to tolerate his sufferings with grace and acceptance. If Job could praise God through all his terrible adversities, then surely Blade could cope with his own problems, which were small in comparison. He had been dealing with his situation with too much hostility, and he vowed to change.

He slowed to a stop and leaned against a tree, catching his breath. The safe house was in sight, its windows glowing with soft light inside. Archie's room was lit with a yellow lamp, and he imagined Josie inside reading their son a bedtime story while Sherbet chirruped away in the corner. It was the scene of idyllic family life that he had been yearning for, but as Josie had rightly pointed out to him, it wasn't real.

Still with a heavy heart, he jogged to the front door and knocked four times, rhythmically and lightly, as they had been instructed. Detective Pullman opened up and ushered him inside. His face was somber.

"I've been waiting for you to get back," the detective said. "I need to speak with you and Josie immediately."

Blade pulled his beanie from his head, feeling steam rising from his curly hair. "What happened?"

"I'd prefer to speak to you together."

"Okay, I'll go get her."

Blade looked up at the closed door of his son's room. He could hear Josie's gentle voice rising and falling with the words of a story. This was intermingled with high-pitched giggles from Archie, who was clearly loving the book.

He started to climb the stairs before remembering the earlier accident and turning around. "By the way, how is Detective Sykes?"

"All good. She has a mild concussion, but she's had a couple of stitches, and she'll be discharged soon. Unsurprisingly, she wants to get straight back on the job, but for tonight the officer who drove you home from Norman's house will replace her."

Blade continued to ascend the stairs, still wearing his running blade. The curved foot bounced on the thick carpet, giving almost soundless movement, and when he gently opened the door to his son's bedroom, Josie looked up in fright.

"Hey," she said with relief. "You startled me."

Archie, wearing pajamas patterned with all kinds of trains, jumped out of bed and gazed, openmouthed, at his father's prosthesis. This was the first time he'd ever seen it attached to Blade's leg.

"Wow!" he exclaimed. "You look like a robot. Can I try it on?"

Blade laughed and sat on a chair in the corner of the room, next to Sherbet's cage, which was covered by a sheet.

"It would be a little big on you, I think," Blade said. "But you can take a look if you like."

Archie raced to his father and dived to the carpet, running his eyes up and down the prosthesis, seemingly transfixed.

Blade tapped the false limb with his finger. "This is made from the same type of stuff used to make baseball bats and bicycles. It's really strong." He stood and bounced up and down. "See?"

"Did you make it yourself?" Archie asked, rubbing at the carbon fiber with his finger.

"Oh, no," Blade replied. "Some very smart people made this especially for me, and it cost a lot of money."

"How much?"

"Fifteen thousand dollars."

Blade heard Josie gasp from her seated position on the bed. Most people rarely appreciated the high cost of good-quality mobility equipment. Yet fifteen grand was a small price to pay for a prosthesis that had transformed his life. He would have paid double.

Josie stood and guided Archie back into bed.

"Can I come watch you in the special games?" Archie asked as his mother tucked him in. "How far do you run in your races?"

"I run three different distances," Blade said. "The one hundred, two hundred and four hundred meters. I'll be competing in a few months." He didn't look at Josie, deciding that he didn't need her permission to take his son along to the most important event of his life so far. "Sure, you can come. I have a bunch of friends who can sit with you in the stadium. You'll like them a lot."

Josie said nothing to challenge him. She kissed Archie on the forehead, switched off the bedside lamp, flipped the switch of a plug-in night-light and walked over to the open door.

"I think I'll go to bed, too," she said with a yawn. "It's another big day tomorrow."

Blade joined her in the hallway. "Detective Pullman would like to speak to us downstairs," he whispered. "It sounds important."

Josie checked her watch and sighed. Her translucent skin had lost its sheen, and he saw the faint outline of circles beneath her eyes. He hated the way his mind told him to wrap his arms around her. It wasn't what either of them wanted.

Instead he reached for the knob of Archie's bedroom door and said, "Good night, son," before softly clicking it closed.

Then he faced Josie. "Did you call your aunt Susan?"

She ran her hands through her long hair, gathering it up and securing it with a band from around her wrist. "Yes, I did. She's on a cruise in the Gulf of Mexico."

"I see," he said, fighting the urge to smile. "So I guess Archie stays here with us?"

"Yes, for the time being." She started to descend the stairs. "But I'm going to call my grandparents in Dodge City. It's closer than I would like him to be to the danger, but it looks like the only alternative."

Blade followed in her footsteps, but he didn't see the toy car that Archie had left on a stair. His foot slid on the wheels and he stumbled, grasping the handrail to balance himself. Josie stopped and turned around.

He expected an immediate offer of assistance and preempted it by saying, "I'm okay. I don't need help."

"I know," she said, bending down to pick up the toy car. "I've slipped on these things a hundred times. I keep telling Archie how dangerous it is, but he never learns."

Then she turned her back and walked away.

She didn't offer him her arm for support or even watch him descend to make sure he made it to the bottom safely. She disappeared into the living room, allowing him to make his own way. She seemed to have gotten the message, following up her apology with a real change in her behavior. It was a small victory, but it meant the world to him.

When he entered the living room, Detective Pullman was seated on the couch, holding a photograph in his hands. The anxious expression on his face added years to his youthful face. "Take a seat," the detective said, gesturing to the couch where Josie was already settled. "I have some news about the man you asked me to check out in the Lansing Correctional Facility."

"Orlando Cardwell," Josie said, suddenly interested. "What did he say?"

"We didn't manage to speak with him."

"So, why are we here?" Blade asked. "You implied this was urgent."

"It *is* urgent," Detective Pullman said. "I just found out that Mr. Cardwell broke out of prison over two months ago."

EIGHT

Josie immediately leaped from the sofa.

"What?" She began to pace. "How did this happen?"

"Details of the escape aren't absolutely clear," Detective Pullman replied. "But a prison guard was found murdered in Mr. Cardwell's cell the morning after his night shift. The guard's keys were missing, and so was Orlando Cardwell. He's been on the run ever since, living rough, reportedly hanging out with homeless people, blending into the background wherever he goes."

Josie stopped pacing as an imaginary light-bulb switched on in her mind.

"It was the eyes!" she exclaimed. "The man in the courtroom had eyes that I should've known immediately. It was Cardwell."

She shook her head, admonishing herself for failing to recognize Cardwell's cold, hard gaze, devoid of any kindness or compassion. She had only ever known Orlando Cardwell to be immaculately dressed in expensive suits, shoes buffed to a shine, with his hair always perfectly coiffured. The scruffy, bearded man sitting in the third row was a world away from the spotless, yet deeply unpleasant, client she had known. He had fooled her.

"It's him, isn't it?" she asked, sitting down next to Blade. "It's Cardwell who's been stalking me."

Detective Pullman nodded solemnly. "The police are assuming so. They interviewed some of his fellow inmates, who confirm that Cardwell held a lot of hatred for you, Josie. He seems to have focused all his bitterness and anger on you, blaming you for his disastrous trial and long sentence."

"That sounds like Cardwell," Josie said, raising her eyes to the ceiling. "It's always somebody else's fault."

As Josie leaned forward, she felt Blade's hand rest on her back and rub gently between her shoulders. She was surprised he was making such an affectionate gesture after their heated argument. But she needed to feel a comforting touch, and she was glad he was adult enough to put their squabble behind them.

"Why didn't the authorities contact Josie and tell her about Cardwell's escape?" Blade asked. "She should have been one of the first to know."

"The breakout has been kept under wraps," Detective Pullman replied. "The US Marshals thought they had a good chance of recapturing him by monitoring the homeless communities where he hangs out. They didn't want to spook him into fleeing Kansas by splashing his face all over the news."

"But the marshals haven't found him, have they?" Josie retorted. "He's in Sedgwick, and he's hunting me."

"Unfortunately, Cardwell seems to be quite a slippery character," the detective said. "The marshals have been focusing their efforts on the Topeka area, where he was thought to be hiding. Since they've been made aware of the threats on your life, two marshals have been sent to Sedgwick to flush him out."

Josie placed a hand across her stomach, where a sensation of sickness had settled. She wondered how long Cardwell had been watching her, how often he had watched her son. It was a heart-stopping thought, reminding her of how dangerous this situation was for Archie. Much as she didn't want to resurrect their disastrous earlier conversation, Josie would have to speak to Blade again about sending Archie away. She would have to make him see that she knew best.

"Will marshals be coming here?" Blade asked.

"No," Detective Pullman said. "The last thing

we want to do is draw attention to ourselves, so we'll keep activity here to a minimum. Otherwise the neighbors might start to wonder what's going on."

Josie looked around the room with its bare, pale walls and bland furnishings. At that moment she yearned to be at her own home with its happy memories and familiar possessions. She was beginning to hate this house. Despite its size, it sometimes gave her a sensation of claustrophobia. Yet she wasn't sure how much of this feeling was also caused by Blade. His presence often brought on a shortness of breath and a desire to run outside for air. She didn't seem to be in control of her emotions while he was around.

"If Cardwell can slip through the marshals' net so easily, then I guess he could find us here," she said. "Maybe we should leave."

"That won't be necessary," the detective said. "There's no reason to suspect that Cardwell will locate you here. We have procedures in place to make sure he can't follow us, and moving would only place further strain on your family."

Josie rubbed her eyes. She was like a parched flower in need of water. She wanted to flourish again, and sleep soundly through the night. After only four nights in the safe house, she was about ready to go to bed for a whole week.

"I think I'd like to go home," she said quietly. "I need my own bed."

Blade removed his hand from her back and placed it on his knee. "What about Archie?" he asked quietly. "Do you think it's safe for him to return home?"

"No, of course not. Like I said, I'll be asking my dad to drive Archie to my grandparents' house in Dodge City. I'd rather he went out of state, but at least Dodge City is one hundred fifty miles from Wichita." She ignored the unwavering stare coming from Blade. "Archie loves his great-gramps, and I'm sure my dad would like to spend some time with his parents, so it could work out well."

Blade looked at Detective Pullman. "Could you give us a few minutes to talk?"

The detective seemed already to have sensed the need to leave and was in the process of rising from the couch. Both Detectives Pullman and Sykes were becoming very perceptive where Josie and Blade were concerned, often slipping out of the room when tensions rose.

"Sure," he said, making his way out of the room. "But think carefully about leaving this house, Josie. I know you're homesick, but you're safe."

Once he was gone, Blade wasted no time in saying what was on his mind.

"You drive me crazy sometimes, you know that? I want to be friends with you, but you won't let me."

Josie crossed her arms. She had no intention of being drawn into another argument. "I'm tired. I'm going to bed."

"Why don't you trust me to make good choices for Archie?" Blade asked. "Is it because of my disability?"

"No," she said quickly. "Your missing limb has no effect on your ability to be a good dad." Now she was caught up in a conversation that she didn't want to have, but she needed to continue. "I've already apologized for my insensitive offers of help, and I hope we can put it behind us. Your disability was never the reason for my lack of trust in you."

"So, what is the real cause? Is it because I'm a little more rough and ready with Archie than you are?"

"Archie is still so young, but you've already talked about letting him swim in the deep end of the pool and climb higher than I think is safe." Josie clenched her fists tight. "I just don't think you see the danger. Maybe it's because you're a former SEAL."

"Or maybe it's because I'm a dad," he said. "Maybe there's a simpler explanation for our dif-

ference of opinion. You're a mom and I'm a dad
We have different roles to play."

Josie snorted. "I hardly think that our gender
is relevant here."

"Think about it, Josie," Blade said. "When
you were growing up, who encouraged you to
climb the tree in your backyard? And who came
running to see to your cut knees and elbows
when you fell?"

Josie fell silent. Blade knew of her childhood
in Sedgwick, of the huge oak tree in the yard
where she and her dad built a tree house. She suffered many cuts and scrapes when she was a kid,
but her mom would clean and dress the wounds
so she could go straight back outside and continue playing. She had always been tough, even
as a child, and nothing kept her down for long.

It infuriated her, but Blade was right. Her father would be the one encouraging her to climb
higher, whereas her mom would yell for her to
come down.

"My situation was different," she said after a
few seconds of silence, trying to create a coun-
terargument in her mind. "Archie and I are total
opposites. I was a tomboy, but he's a sweet and
gentle kid who needs a lot of support."

Blade threw his head back with a sound of
disbelief.

"Are you kidding me?" he said with a laugh.

"He's the toughest kid I ever met." He pointed to the sturdy light fixture in the center of the ceiling. "I found him dangling upside down from that yesterday."

Josie gasped. Blade hadn't told her this.

He seemed to read her mind. "I gave him a lecture and made him promise never to do it again, but it just goes to prove how fearless he is. He needs somebody to help him channel that desire for adventure." He took a deep breath. "He needs *me*."

"Archie never used to be this way until you came into his life," Josie said, trying not to imagine her son falling from the light fixture and onto the coffee table. "He used to be much calmer and quieter. But he prefers spending time with you now, and I can't do anything about it. He's changed."

"Do you think I'm a bad influence?"

Josie really didn't want to answer that question, but she couldn't evade it. "Sometimes."

"Josie, listen to me," he said earnestly, taking her hand. "We have a beautiful son who's never had the freedom to play rough. He's always tried to please you by being the kind of calm and quiet child you expect him to be. Just because he enjoys spending time with me doesn't mean you're losing him to me. The truth is, he's a high-spirited boy, and you have to let him explore different sides of his character."

She slid her hand from beneath his. She felt as though Blade was lecturing her, trying to make her feel like a poor mother for protecting her son from harm.

"Why are we even talking about this?" she said irritably. "Is it because you don't want him to go and stay in Dodge City?"

Blade was amicable in his reply. "Actually, I've come around to your way of thinking on this. Archie is going stir-crazy cooped up here." As if to emphasize his point, his eyes flicked to the light fixture. "Giving him the freedom to play outdoors away from here seems like a great idea, but I wish we'd decided on this course of action mutually. You have to stop shutting me out of parenting."

"I don't shut you out," she protested, but there was no conviction in her voice. She stood. "I really have to go to my room now, although I doubt I'll get a good night's sleep. This place just doesn't suit me. I'd prefer to be in my own bed."

He rose to stand with her. "I know it's hard to fight the instinct to rush back home when you're tired and low, but sleep on it. We'll talk again in the morning and make arrangements for your dad and Archie to travel to Dodge City."

Then he leaned forward and gave her a kiss

on the cheek, as if it were the most normal thing in the world. "Try not to worry," he said. "We'll figure this out together."

She took a step back from him, shocked at the tenderness of his touch, and surprised at the warm glow it was spreading across her skin. She headed for the stairs, confused and embarrassed, rubbing the cheek where Blade's lips had just been.

His touch seemed to have awakened an old ache in her heart, prompting her to think of the months she'd spent longing to see him just one more time.

But she was a different woman now, and she could not go back there again.

Blade tried to shield Josie as best he could as they approached the courthouse, battling their way through TV crews and protesters. The protest against Norman using the public defender's office had grown since the local news stations had picked up the story. All kinds of falsehoods and misinformation had suddenly been accepted as true by the public. Norman was thought to be hiding ninety thousand dollars in cash, and now he was being accused of loitering outside schools and playgrounds. These claims were very easy to make but impossible to verify, so Norman was at the mercy of cruel gossipers.

"Stand aside," Detective Pullman ordered as they approached the entrance. "Don't make me arrest any of you."

A microphone was thrust under Josie's nose, rapid-fire questions thrown at her. Blade put out a hand and pushed the microphone away. With so much activity, it was impossible to scan the area for Cardwell. He just had to hope that the two US marshals were doing an adequate job from their positions around the building.

Entering the courthouse was like stepping into an oasis of calm. The reverent hush was wonderful, and Blade, Josie and Detective Pullman took a few seconds to absorb the atmosphere before going through security.

"This is crazy," Josie said, placing her briefcase and laptop on the belt for scanning. "I've never seen anything like it."

"It seems like the media is whipping the public up into a frenzy," Detective Pullman said, handing his weapon over for inspection. "They're vilifying Norman."

Blade also handed over his weapon. However, unlike Detective Pullman, he would not be receiving his back until he left the building. "Norman is an easy target, I guess," he said. "He doesn't fit the stereotype of the all-American man. He's small, reclusive and unusual-looking."

Josie pursed her lips and exhaled through

her nostrils, clearly annoyed. "Once the spark of gossip catches, it doesn't take long for the flames to take hold. It takes only one match to burn a whole forest."

Josie picked up her bags and walked into the large foyer. Today she was wearing a vivid red pantsuit with matching shoes. Her hair was pinned into another tight bun, exposing her high cheekbones and ruby lips.

He smiled at her. He had decided that, since his recent attempts at conversation had led to nothing but acrimony, he would try constant kindness. He knew that Josie's animosity toward him was based on nothing more than fear of losing Archie, both emotionally and physically. Not only was Archie asserting his independence from his mother, but also he was doing more daring activities, encouraged and supported by his father. Blade was intelligent enough to realize that Josie wasn't truly angry with him. She was simply afraid. And looking at her standing in the hallway, poised and collected in her body-skimming suit, he felt a sense of dread in his heart, also. He was growing closer to her, enjoying her company and feeling more protective of her each day. Much to his amazement— and despite their arguments over how to parent Archie—he was close to falling in love with her all over again.

Shaking this thought away, he said, "Red is the color of success, you know that? You look great."

She smoothed down her jacket, looking surprisingly coy about receiving a compliment from him. "Thank you."

The next voice that cut through the air caused a groan to come from Josie's lips.

"I agree with your SEAL friend, Josie," Allan Sanders said, striding across the marble floor. "You look fantastic." He approached and shook her hand in a formal and stiff gesture. "You've got yourself all dolled up for the big day today, huh?" He beamed, performing a jazz-hands movement. "It's showtime."

"I hardly think we should be comparing the courtroom to a stage performance," Josie said, not bothering to hide her irritation. "A man's future is at stake here."

Allan folded his arms across his gray suit jacket. "Ah, yes, it's such a shame about the negative news coverage regarding your client, isn't it?" Blade noticed that the prosecutor had a copy of the *Sedgwick Chronicle* tucked beneath his armpit. "But what can you expect when you're representing a child predator?"

"I think I've heard enough," Blade said, stepping forward. This was getting too personal for his liking. "Norman Francis is a good and decent man, and I think he should be afforded a little more respect."

Allan raised his head in an attempt to look down on Blade, but his average height wouldn't allow it. "I give Norman Francis as much respect as he deserves," he said with a faint sneer. "Once you hear the testimony of Janice Weeks, today I think you might be ready to change your mind about Mr. Francis. His *little boy lost* routine might have worked on you, but it doesn't fool me."

Blade felt Josie's fingers curl around his wrist.

"Your conduct is totally unethical, Allan," she said, leading Blade a few paces away. "Norman is my client, and your attempt to smear his good character in front of others is quite devious. Let's save this for the courtroom, where it belongs."

Allan smiled. "You're absolutely right, Josie. You've always been my favorite defense attorney, even if your decision to continue this trial is rather reckless. Putting yourself in the line of fire after receiving death threats isn't one of your better choices."

He turned to walk away, before obviously remembering something important and spinning around with a raised index finger in the air. "Oh, I almost forgot. You might not have heard that we're in a different courtroom today. Another bomb scare was received this morning. A hoax, of course, but the judge decided not to take any chances, so he's commandeered another court-room. The judge himself will furnish you with all the details."

"I don't believe it," Josie said to Blade, staring openmouthed at the back of Allan Sanders as he ran up the stairs, bouncing on the balls of his feet like a boxer preparing for a fight. "He just dropped that piece of information into the con-versation like he was discussing the weather." She shook her head, wide-eyed and shocked. "Another bomb hoax. It's obviously Cardwell's way of causing me maximum fear." She adjusted the collar of her crisp white blouse. "I guess I'll have to get used to it."

Blade glanced over at Detective Pullman, who was deep in conversation with one of the se-curity officers, no doubt gleaning all the facts about the bomb hoax. He then led Josie to a quiet corner and pulled her into his arms. He sensed a resistance at first, but she quickly ac-cepted his affection and allowed her body to go limp, holding her briefcase with one hand and sliding the other around his waist. Her forehead rested lightly on his chest, rising and falling with his breathing, and she said nothing for a while. When she drew away, he saw that her color had paled and her eyes had begun to water.

"Thank you," she said quietly. "I appreciate

the support you're giving me even though we fight a lot."

"We don't fight," he said with a smile. "We disagree. It's different."

She laughed lightly. "Well, whatever you want to call it, you haven't let it make you bitter. You've been really kind to me, and sometimes I feel like I don't deserve it, especially after I made such a mess of dealing with your disability."

He waved his hand through the air. "It's all forgotten. However much we fight—" He stopped to correct himself. "However much we *disagree*, I will always care about you and always protect you. You're the mother of my child and the only woman who's ever meant anything to me."

Josie swallowed hard as her eyes gathered more moisture.

He continued speaking in a hushed tone in the quiet foyer. "It's not good for Archie to see tension between us, so I promise not to get angry or raise my voice to you. That's no way for a man to treat a woman, anyway. If we're going to resolve our differences, the only way forward is to be kind to one another." He touched her cheek. It was cool and smooth. "Always."

She nodded, seemingly unwilling or unable to speak.

"Now, let's go and find your client," he said.

"You've got a big day ahead, and you need to be mentally strong." He squeezed her hand. "You ready to win this trial?"

She gave his hand a reciprocal squeeze. "Ready."

"I'll be right behind you," he said. "If you need me or you feel unsafe, just turn around to face me and hold up your index finger. That'll be our signal."

She held up her finger. "Got it."

He gave her one last hug, enjoying it far more than he should have. That conversation had served to draw his heart even closer to hers. Kindness was the only way forward, and they had now agreed to treat each other with mutual respect.

He just hoped she would be able to hold up her end of the bargain.

Josie rose from her chair, her legs slightly shaky and her palms sweaty. Allan Sanders was leaning back in his chair, a self-satisfied smile on his face, having just displayed his superb skills as a prosecutor. His interviewing of Janice Weeks was impressive, clever and persuasive. He had presented Janice as someone of high standing in the community, respected and honest, as well as a decent, churchgoing woman. As a result, her testimony had been powerful, and

Josie noticed the jury hanging on her every word as she told them of Norman's approach to little Lisa and his guiding her into his home. Josie was now facing an uphill battle in her cross-examination.

"Miss Weeks," she began, "how long have you known Norman Francis?"

Janice answered quickly, as if she had rehearsed the obvious questions. "Three years. I met him when I moved into the house next door."

Josie smiled. "It's a nice, quiet street, from what I know of it. Do you enjoy living there?"

Janice narrowed her eyes suspiciously. "It's all right. Mostly I like it."

"Mostly?" Josie repeated. "But not always?"

"Nowhere is perfect," Janice replied crisply.

"I agree, Miss Weeks," Josie said. "Small things can spoil an idyllic neighborhood, can't they?" She raised her eyebrows. "Such as having an irritating neighbor. Do you have good relationships with your neighbors?"

As Josie had expected, Allan Sanders leaped to his feet. "Objection—immaterial."

Josie faced the judge. "Your Honor, Miss Weeks's relationship with Norman Francis, one of her neighbors, is very important. We must establish whether she has a motive to lie or exaggerate about what she saw."

The judge nodded, his jowly, craggy face

bathed in sunlight from the window. "I'll allow it, but be careful, Counselor, and stick to her relationship with Mr. Francis only."

Josie accepted this ruling with gratitude. That suited her just fine. As she sidestepped away from her chair, taking her time to gather her thoughts, she glanced behind and caught sight of Blade. He was standing tall and erect near the exit, arms folded, watching the proceedings intently. His mop of sandy hair stood above all else, and his deep-set eyes were almost impossible to see beneath his furrowed brow.

It seemed ridiculous to Josie that she had ever thought Blade's disability would prevent him from standing for long periods. It seemed even more ridiculous that she believed he needed her help to compensate for his missing limb. He was strong and capable and steadfast. A pang of shame pierced her belly. Whatever reservations she'd had about his parenting of Archie, she should never have doubted him as a protector and bodyguard.

Come on, Josie, she told herself silently. *Keep your focus on the witness.*

"Is it true, Miss Weeks," she began, deciding to come right out with what she wanted to probe, "that you and Norman Francis have a long-running feud regarding the persistent barking and howling of your pet dogs?"

Janice pinched her lips into a thin smile. She was a woman of fifty but looked much older, with hair set firm with hair spray and heavily applied spots of blush on her cheeks. She had the appearance of a sun lover, and a deep tan accentuated the lines around her mouth and eyes.

"I would hardly call it a feud," Janice replied tersely. "Norman complained about my dogs' barking a couple of times."

"A couple of times?" Josie repeated. She checked her notes. "In fact, Norman Francis complained to Animal Control a total of twenty-three times over the course of two years, did he not?"

Janice shifted uncomfortably in her seat. "I don't recall how many times it was."

"And during those two years," Josie continued, "Animal Control repeatedly warned you about your dogs' barking and howling. In fact, you have been issued a number of fines, am I right?"

Josie noticed Allan Sanders's leg twitching as if he wanted to jump up and object, but he knew he would be overruled. The bad blood between Janice and Norman was highly relevant.

"They're basset hounds," Janice said, throwing a wide smile at the jury. "They like to talk." Her smile vanished when she turned her attention back to Josie. "Norman just isn't a dog person."

"Please answer the question, Miss Weeks," Josie said, ignoring Janice's attempt to sidetrack the jury. "Has Animal Control fined you for failing to curb the noise of your pet dogs?" She checked her notes again. "They've visited you twelve times, according to their records. Would you concur?"

Finally the answer came. "Yes."

Before Josie could ask another question, Janice appeared to drop her mask of respectability, and her stony face reddened. She pointed to Norman, who was sitting hunched over, making himself as inconspicuous as possible.

"Instead of bombarding me with stupid questions, why don't you ask him what happened to Buster? Go on, ask him. Let's see what he has to say."

Josie watched the spittle gather at the corners of Janice's mouth. She was losing her cool. Allan Sanders could see it also and flew to his feet.

"Would the court entertain a request for a brief recess?" he asked, staring imploringly at Janice, clearly trying to drag her back on track.

The judge settled his eyes on Josie. "Do you object to this request, Counselor?"

"I most certainly do, Your Honor. I would prefer to continue my immediate questioning of this vital witness."

The judge nodded his approval. "Your request

is denied, Mr. Sanders. The defense counsel may proceed."

Josie wasted no time in continuing. "Miss Weeks, may I ask who Buster is?"

"He's one of my dogs," Janice replied, her eyes watering. "Or rather, he *was* one of my dogs. I found him dead not long after I moved into the house next door to Norman." She flared her nostrils as if a strong smell had reached her nose. "The vet said it was poison."

Josie watched Allan Sanders put his head in his hands. This testimony was suddenly not looking so airtight.

Josie already knew the answer to her next question, and ideally, so would the jury.

"Why would you like me to ask Mr. Francis what happened to Buster?"

Janice locked eyes with Sanders and seemed to rally herself, taking heed of the prosecutor's warning glance.

"I…um… I thought he might know who did it," Janice replied nervously, tucking stiff hair behind her ears. "He knows a lot of people in the neighborhood, so I figured he would have a better idea than me."

"But, Miss Weeks, you said yourself that Buster was poisoned shortly after you moved next door to Norman, which was three years ago. Why wait until you are sitting in a packed courtroom, giving important witness testimony, to ask this question of Norman? Why didn't you ask him immediately after the incident?"

"I don't know," Janice said, regaining her composure. "This is a very nerve-racking experience." Once again, she turned her head and smiled at the jury. "My mind isn't thinking straight. I'm sorry for veering off track. Buster's death upset me deeply."

When she turned back to Josie, she appeared to be fully in control of her wayward emotions, and Josie began to panic that the defense had lost momentum. Then an idea struck her. Norman had not yet given her permission to divulge his disability to the courtroom, but it might be necessary in order to prove that Janice's witness statement was untrue. She desperately hoped that Norman would understand.

"Miss Weeks," Josie said, "you claim that you saw Norman lead Lisa Brown into his home by the hand. Is that correct?"

"Correct."

"Do you recall what hand Norman used to do this?"

Janice cocked her head to the side, wondering why this information was important. She must have decided that it held no relevance. "His right hand."

Josie felt a surge of excitement but remained impassive. "Are you absolutely sure about that?"

Janice closed her eyes, making a great pretense of remembering the incident. "I recall seeing Norman drag the girl up the path from my bedroom window. His back was turned to me, so from the angle I was watching, he must have been using his right hand to pull the girl behind him." She smiled triumphantly, as if she had successfully backed up her memory with solid detail. "Yes, I'm sure of it. He had a good tight hold of her, too."

Josie placed a hand on her client's shoulder. "Can you stand up and remove your overcoat please, Norman?"

Norman snapped his head up to look at her sharply, his eyes showing hesitation. "Trust me," she whispered, helping him to his feet. "This is the only way.

"It may surprise you to learn that Norman Francis suffers from a condition called cerebral palsy," she said, slipping her client's arms through his sleeves. "His right arm has virtually no strength or mobility at all."

She stepped back to allow the witness and the jury to see Norman's arm hanging limply inside his shirtsleeve, and a collective gasp was audible around the courtroom. Allan Sanders gave a small shake of his head and rubbed at his temples. As the prosecutor, he had been privy to Norman's medical details, but Janice had not, and Sanders had been unable to warn his star witness of this potential complication due to the judge's ruling on maintaining confidentiality.

Josie continued. "I'm afraid there is no way Norman could grip anyone's hand, even that of a three-year-old girl, let alone drag her along a path. Maybe you are mistaken in your testimony, Miss Weeks, because it is entirely untrue."

"Objection!"

Allan Sanders's voice was loud and clear, but it was quickly drowned out by that of Janice Weeks, whose mask of calm once again slipped. This time it slid off entirely, revealing a face of unfettered anger.

"He did it!" she shrieked. "Just look at him. Of course he did it. He's a dirty old man, walking around in that coat all the time. My friend Penny told me he exposed himself to her in the local park."

Snickers and open laughter rippled around the court. Josie heard the prosecutor's voice trying to rise above the noise. "Permission to approach the bench, Your Honor?"

But Janice wasn't done yet and launched into another tirade. "And he poisoned my dog. I'm sure of it. I don't believe he has any disease or condition or whatever you call it. I think he's a fake and a phony, trying to get sympathy. He's a nasty, horrible weirdo. I can't stand living next door to him."

The noise in the courtroom escalated as the people in the gallery began to speak openly to each other. The judge called for order as the prosecutor repeated his request to approach the bench. Yet the judge was too focused on bringing his courtroom back under control.

Josie needed to strike now, before proceedings were halted. She spoke over Allan Sanders's request, knowing he was preparing to argue that his witness required a break.

"Miss Weeks, did you see Norman Francis take Lisa Brown into his home, yes or no?"

Janice spit out her reply, unleashing the venom she held for her elderly neighbor. "I saw that sweet girl skip right into his house all by herself. Poor little thing had no idea what kind of place she was walking into." She pointed at Norman. "It's obvious he'd bribed her inside somehow, but I had to embellish the details to make the police come quick. If I hadn't called the cops, who knows what would've happened. I saved her. You should be thanking me."

Josie raised her voice to a shout. "Please respond to the question with a yes or no answer. Did you see Norman Francis lead Lisa Brown into his home?"

Janice looked her squarely in the eye. "No, but he's guilty anyway."

With that, the courtroom erupted in shouts and calls, mingled with exclamations of surprise and horror from Lisa's family.

Josie was elated, but she kept the presence of mind to do what was necessary.

"Your Honor," she shouted above the noise. "I would like to make a motion to dismiss the charges against my client."

Then she turned to smile at Blade. This was the perfect day so far. Everything had gone her way.

Yet her smile was short-lived. And in the next moment, her index finger went up into the air just as she and Blade had agreed.

NINE

Blade reacted immediately, following Josie's pointing finger, leading his eyes toward a backpack leaning against the wall in the corner of the courtroom. The bag was jet-black, innocuous enough except for the wires peeking out from the top.

Blade scanned the area around the bag, seeing nobody standing near it. Josie stood immobile, staring at it, clearly spooked by its presence. And she was right to be afraid. Whether this was the real deal or not was irrelevant. The courtroom should be evacuated. Immediately.

With no time to lose, Blade rushed to the nearest security officer. The judge was still struggling to retain order in his court as people refused to quiet down. The high emotion surrounding this case was spilling out from all directions, and the disappointment from little Lisa's family could be heard in their continued cries and gasps.

When Blade spoke quietly to the officer, giving him details of the suspicious backpack, he was acutely aware of the need to prevent panic from breaking out. If these people thought they might be in imminent danger from a bomb, there would be a stampede. The security officer walked purposefully to the judge and leaned to whisper in his ear. All the while, Blade kept his eyes on Josie, trying to reassure her with a calm expression. Her euphoria at exposing Janice Weeks as a malicious liar had been snatched away, and Blade was angry on her behalf. One of the greatest moments in her career would now be tarnished by Cardwell and his campaign of hate.

He watched Josie help Norman put his coat back on as the judge announced that the court was now in recess and would be immediately evacuated due to a possible threat. Dismissing Janice Weeks from the witness stand, the judge rose from his chair and began to oversee the emptying of his courtroom.

Blade fought against the flow of people heading for the exit door and reached Josie's side as she was cramming her notes into her briefcase.

"Let's go," he said, placing a hand on her shoulder. "It's probably another hoax, but we don't want to take any chances."

"We need to protect Norman," she said, beckoning a security officer to come to their aid.

"He's too frail to go out the main exit with all these people. We'll use the side door."

Blade looked at the door she was indicating just in time to see Allan Sanders rushing through it with Janice Weeks. His face was a mixture of anger and defeat. After the disastrous performance of his most important witness, he must now know that the case was lost.

The officer appeared at their side.

"Please escort my client to a place of safety," Josie said briskly, ushering Norman toward him. "Norman, I'll meet you out back."

The jury was filing out of their seats, disappearing one by one through another side door. The courtroom was emptying pretty fast, and Blade started to feel more anxious.

"Come on, Josie," he said. "We're almost the last ones here."

"Don't panic," she said, grabbing her briefcase. "This is the third bomb scare this week, and the other two have both been hoaxes. This one is likely to be no different."

Blade took her hand. "Let's not take a chance on that."

Together they headed for the exit, joining the last of the people heading out the main door, being guided by a security officer. The bottleneck created by the sudden emptying of the court meant that the pace was slow, and this was clearly causing concern for the officer.

"Let's go a little faster, folks," he called. "No need to panic, but move along now."

Josie turned to look at the bag as she passed, and Blade began to steer her to his right side, away from the danger.

"I must admit," she said with a note of what sounded like admiration, "Cardwell's made an impressive fake. It could almost be the real deal."

Then, as if to mock her words, the room was rocked by an explosion that seemed to hit them with the force of a volcano.

Blade struggled to breathe as thick, acrid smoke choked his lungs. The wailing screech of the fire alarm seemed to be piercing his eardrums, and he fought the sensation of dizziness, staggering to his feet and shaking the dust from his hair.

"Josie!" he yelled. "Josie, where are you?"

The room was damaged most heavily where the bomb had been located. That wall was now partially collapsed, and the chairs of the public gallery were strewn in all directions. The impact on Blade and Josie had come from the shock wave, knocking them right off their feet.

"Josie!" he yelled again. Why couldn't he see her? She had vanished.

All he could see in the dusty gloom were a handful of other people who had also been exiting the courtroom, wandering dazed and confused, but largely unharmed. It had been Josie who'd taken the brunt of the blast. Why hadn't Blade steered her away from the bag quicker? He should've placed himself between her and the bomb without delay.

He spun around, light-headedness almost threatening to send him to the floor again. Then he saw Josie's legs protruding from behind the wooden witness stand. She had been blown at least seven feet away. He rushed to her side, only to find her knocked out cold. There was no visible sign of blood, but that couldn't discount internal injuries. Her face was deathly pale, covered with a fine layer of plaster dust, yet she was breathing.

"Can I get some help here?" he bellowed at the top of his voice. "We need an ambulance!"

He brushed the dust from her face, holding two fingers to her neck and taking her pulse. "You'll be okay, Josie," he said softly. "Hold tight."

He looked around to spot the security officer who had been ushering them from the room, but it appeared this man hadn't been so fortunate. His body was lying on the floor, mangled and bloody. Blade closed his eyes and said a prayer for the fallen man before turning his attention back to Josie.

"You did a great job today, honey," he said, daring to speak more intimately while she was in this unconscious state. "I'm so proud of you." He thought of the way she carried herself around the court, poised and elegant, her bright red suit giving her extra gravitas. "You were beautiful out there."

A hand suddenly appeared on his shoulder and pulled him back. He saw a woman in a long skirt and high heels kneel to the floor.

"Who are you?" he asked.

"I'm one of the clerks here, but I'm also trained in first aid." She lifted up one of Josie's eyelids and shone a tiny flashlight into her eye. "What's her name?"

"Josie."

The woman began to speak loudly, tapping Josie's cheek. "Josie. Josie. Can you hear me? Open your eyes if you can." She glanced at Blade. "Paramedics are on their way. They might need some background medical details for her. Are you her husband or boyfriend?"

Blade struggled to shake the feeling that he might lose her. "Neither." He didn't know how to describe their relationship. "I'm just a friend."

The woman checked Josie for broken bones. "Is she allergic to any medications?"

Blade shook his head. "I don't know."

"Does she have any medical conditions that we should know about?"

He wished he had the answers to these questions. "I don't think so, but I'm not sure."

Blade looked on helplessly, realizing how little he knew about the mother of his child. He couldn't even name her favorite color, food or movie. He used to know everything about her, yet he had pushed it into the margins of his memory, along with all the negative emotions he associated with the early days after the loss of his leg. The amputation had caused him to reject his entire life, including the woman he loved, and he suddenly regretted it with every bone in his body. If only he hadn't been so cowardly. If only he'd stuck around and battled through his grief. He had wasted too many years of his life feeling sorry for himself in Florida, shunning society. But God had pulled him through the darkness and provided him with a purpose. Only God had been able to breathe life into his weary spirit. Only God had given him peace.

And if God would grant his prayer and save Josie's life, Blade solemnly promised that he would never fail her in the same way again.

Josie woke in a white room, the clinical brightness of the walls stinging her eyes. Her head throbbed with pain, and she lifted her hand to touch her temple. The last things she remembered were a blinding flash followed by the most incredible hot wind whooshing past her ears.

"Blade," she croaked. "Are you here?"

"I'm here," he said, taking her hand. "Archie and Tim are on their way."

She lifted her head and looked down at herself. She was still wearing the red pantsuit that she had pulled on that very morning, except it was now dirty and streaked with gray dust.

"Water," she gasped.

Blade lifted a cup of water to her lips, and she felt the exquisite coolness of the liquid slip down her throat, soothing the rawness.

"How long was I out?" she asked, letting her head flop back onto the pillow.

"Around forty minutes," he replied. "But you've been murmuring for a while."

A doctor dressed in a white coat entered the room and smiled. "How do you feel, Miss Bishop?"

"Sore," she said as the doctor leaned over the bed and peered into her eyes with a small black instrument.

"My name is Dr. Susan Evans," the middle-aged woman said. "I examined you as soon as the paramedics brought you in, and I'm pleased to say that you have no broken bones and no symptoms of internal bleeding. But you sustained a concussion from a blow to the head, and we'd like to keep you here overnight to monitor your progress. I'll arrange a CT scan." She stood erect, having completed her inspection of Josie's eyes. "A detective from the Wichita PD tells me that you're under their protection." She glanced at Blade. "So your husband can stay here with you if it makes you feel safer."

"I'm not her husband," Blade said. "But I'd like to stay nevertheless."

"It's an unusual situation," the doctor said. "There are two police officers standing guard at the hospital entrance, and a detective is outside in the corridor." She smiled at Josie. "You must be a very important lady."

"She is," Blade confirmed. "Very much so."

A million thoughts raced through Josie's head. Had she really managed to expose the prosecution's star witness as a fraud? Would the judge now grant her motion to dismiss the charges? When would the trial reconvene? Why was Blade the second person to enter her head when she woke up, his face appearing in her mind right after she had thought of Archie's?

Her expression must have revealed her anxieties, as Blade took her hand and squeezed it.

"Try not to think about anything other than recovering," he said. "Everything else can wait."

"I agree," the doctor said, walking to the end of the bed. "Do you have any dizziness, nausea, numbness or tiredness?"

"No," Josie replied. "But my head hurts."

The doctor headed for the door. "I'll go get some painkillers for you. I'll be back soon." She turned with a smile. "So don't go anywhere, okay?"

When the doctor left, Josie shifted on the bed. Her suit jacket had ridden all the way up her back and was bunched uncomfortably between her shoulders. Blade saw her discomfort and gently raised her from the bed to slip her arms from the sleeves.

"Is Norman all right?" she asked. "He didn't get caught up in the blast, did he?"

"He's totally fine," Blade said. "He's at home, but he's called the hospital twice, asking for news of your condition. I called him a few minutes ago and told him that you're doing well. He's really worried about you." He touched her cheek. "I've been really worried about you, too. You gave me quite a scare."

Josie flicked her eyes up and down Blade's frame. His previously white shirt was now flecked with dirt, and his jeans were especially filthy on the knees as if he'd been kneeling in dust. But he didn't have any visible injuries from the explosion.

"What about you?" she asked. "Are you hurt?"

Blade raised an eyebrow and punched his chest lightly with his fist. "I'm made of strong stuff. Nothing can bring me down."

"Well, you *are* part cyborg," she said with a smile. "That makes you a lot stronger than most."

She suddenly realized that Blade might find this comment offensive. "I'm sorry. I didn't think."

Blade laughed. "It's okay, Josie. Jokes about my leg are fine, as long as they focus on the positive. I have no problem being called 'part cyborg.' It makes me kinda cool."

Josie felt a sense of relief. But it was short-lived, because a memory of the explosion forced its way into her mind, and she raised a hand to her forehead to massage away the dull ache.

"How did somebody manage to bring a bomb into the courthouse?" She knew that Blade wouldn't be able to answer this question. At least, not yet. "The security procedures are so tight that not even a lighter can get through."

Blade's stubbly face grew serious. "Detective Pullman told me that they suspect the bomb was a crude homemade device using fertilizer. Fortunately, we were standing far enough away to escape serious injury. The police have no idea how it was smuggled into the building, but they've launched an investigation. None of the security officers remember seeing anybody with that backpack in the courtroom, but sadly, the officer posted at the door is no longer able to tell us anything. He was pronounced dead at the scene."

Josie squeezed her eyes tightly shut. An innocent man had lost his life because of a crazed man set on revenge.

"The location of the bomb suggests that Cardwell wanted to kill indiscriminately," she said. "He doesn't care who gets hurt."

Blade nodded in agreement. "It certainly seems that way. The people in the gallery would've been in the blast zone. Everybody is very grateful that you spotted the bag in time. The officers were obviously too caught up in the court proceedings to notice it."

Josie couldn't recall her cross-examination of Janice Weeks in great detail. It seemed to have gone by in a blur, but she remembered the noise in the court, the judge calling for order and Allan Sanders sitting with his head in his hands as it became apparent that the cornerstone of his case was crumbling away.

"Did Janice Weeks really admit that she lied about seeing Norman take Lisa into his home?" she asked. "Or did I imagine it?"

"You're not imagining it. You did an amazing job," Blade said. "I couldn't take my eyes off you." He looked at the floor, seemingly embarrassed. "I don't think anybody could take their eyes off you."

As Blade settled his unwavering gaze on her, the throbbing in Josie's head was replaced by a tingling in her scalp. Something in his expression had changed. He was looking at her in a different way, and it reminded her of how they used to be. Blade used to maintain eye contact with her for many minutes at a time, letting her know how intimately they were connected. She hadn't seen that look in his eye for seven years, and she didn't know how to react.

As she felt her color rise, the door opened and the doctor returned, her face partially obscured by an enormous bouquet of flowers.

"These just arrived for you, Miss Bishop," Dr. Evans said, placing them on the table at the side of the bed. "I thought I'd bring them straight in. Aren't they beautiful?"

Josie's gaze immediately left Blade's and snapped to the blooms, their colors of red and white reminding her of blood and bandages. Nestled between the stems was a small envelope. Her name was printed on it in red ink.

Blade clearly shared her trepidation. "Do you want me to read the card?"

"No, I got it," she said, sitting up and plucking the tiny envelope between her thumb and forefinger. Then she carefully opened it up and pulled out the card. She had prepared herself for a shock, but she let out a gasp nonetheless.

The message written on it was typed in small, neat letters:

Today was just a rehearsal. Tomorrow you die for real.

Blade saw a look of horror pass over Josie's face and slid the card from her fingers. After reading the hateful message, he took the flowers from her and handed them back to the doctor.

"Who sent these?" he asked. "Do you know?"

The doctor looked confused at the displeasure that this magnificent bouquet had clearly created. "I'm not sure. I'll ask at the front desk."

Blade couldn't bear to look at the flowers, finding it hard to believe that their beauty could provoke such a feeling of disgust. "Can you give them to Detective Dave Pullman out in the corridor? And make sure he reads the card."

"Of course," the doctor said. "Am I to assume that the sender isn't a friend?"

"That's correct," Blade replied. "If any more gifts arrive, they must be screened by Detective Pullman before being allowed into the room."

The doctor placed a pack of painkillers on the bedside table. "Take two of these to help with your headache. I'll go speak with the detective and come right back."

Blade watched the bouquet disappear through the door and pulled a chair close to Josie's bed. "He won't get a chance to hurt you," he said. "I promise."

Josie either couldn't or wouldn't speak. She blinked quickly while staring upward.

"Hey," he said gently, holding her hand. "Let's remember the positive aspects of today. You ruled that courtroom this morning. You exposed a witness as a fraud and a liar and probably prevented a serious miscarriage of justice as a result."

Josie's lip wobbled slightly. "The judge hasn't dismissed the charges yet. Norman isn't out of the woods. And no matter what happens in the courtroom, it won't stop Cardwell, will it?"

"US marshals are here in Wichita looking for him, and you have round-the-clock protection, including mine." Blade wondered what was going through Josie's mind. She seemed to be in a state of shock, which was hardly surprising under the circumstances, yet he had become used to seeing her so strong and confident.

"Archie needs to leave Wichita," she said quietly. "Today."

Blade had been thinking the same thing. "I

agree. After he and Tim visit you, I'll ask Detective Pullman to drive them to Dodge City."

"I'd like to go back to the safe house with Archie and help him pack a bag," Josie said, reaching for the painkillers.

Blade handed her a glass of water to help her swallow the pills. "You heard what the doctor said. They'd like to keep you here overnight. You have a concussion."

Josie snapped back her head and swallowed both pills with one gulp of water. Then she swung her legs over the side of the bed and took a couple of deep breaths. She was rallying herself. He could see it in her expression, which was resolute and determined, trying to chase away the fear.

"Archie will need me," she said. "I don't know how long he'll be away, and he might forget all the important things, like Oscar."

Blade struggled to place the name. "Oscar?"

"His toy dog. He can't cope if he doesn't have Oscar. He also has a favorite blanket and book." She stood up, wobbling slightly. "Oh, I almost forgot. He uses a special cup for his bedtime drink. He won't go to bed unless he has it. I just don't trust my dad to remember to look for all these things."

Blade took hold of her hand and she struggled to stay steady on her feet. The boy she was describing wasn't the boy he had gotten to know in recent days. Archie was a carefree kid who didn't require any routines to keep him happy. But trying to tell Josie this was like navigating a minefield. Nevertheless, he had to try for their son's sake.

"Archie isn't a toddler anymore, Josie," he said, guiding her to sit back on the bed. "He doesn't need all those things anymore. He'll be just fine. As long as he remembers to take Sherbet, he'll have a great time."

Josie clicked her tongue in an expression of annoyance and irritation. "I know exactly how you feel about my mothering," she said, shuffling herself along the bed, away from him. "I don't think I'm being overprotective or indulgent. Archie is still only six years old."

Blade imagined his six-year-old self, building forts in the woods with his friends, running barefoot through fields of corn, swinging from a rope over the river before plunging headfirst into the cool water. The joy that came with long summer days spent surrounded by nature was unparalleled. By the time Blade was ten, he was able to identify different types of trees and birds, knew what berries were safe to eat, had made a simple crossbow from wood and understood basic survival skills. It was a childhood that set him up for manhood. He couldn't see the point in growing older if his hands weren't calloused and well used. Josie obviously saw Archie's childhood mapped out differently, and he had to tread very carefully so as not to offend her, especially considering the stress she was facing.

"Josie," he said, looking her straight in the eye. Her face was streaked with dirt, but her green eyes shone fiercely through the grime. "I don't think you're overprotective. I think you're a great mom. I honestly do. Archie is the most wonderful child in the world, and I thank God for giving him a mother like you." He placed a hand over his heart as an unexpected well of sentiment bubbled up. His vow to treat Josie with constant kindness seemed to be making him more prone to displays of emotion. "You took care of him unfailingly while I ran away from society like a coward because I lost a leg. You stepped up, carved out a career as a respected defense attorney and raised a wonderful child. So please don't ever think I'm criticizing you. That's the last thing I want to do."

She gave him a sideways look, cautious but friendly. "Thank you."

Now for the hard bit. "But I think that some part of you doesn't want Archie to grow up because you don't want to lose that bond you have. He's your special little boy, and you want to keep him close. You want him to cuddle up to you with his favorite blanket and nighttime sippy cup, just like it's always been since he was a baby, but all children change as they grow up. It's inevitable."

Her friendly expression grew more guarded. "I don't think you know Archie as well as I do." There was something patronizing about her tone that infuriated Blade, but he remembered his promise to be kind. "It'll take you a long time to understand his little quirks and habits," she continued. "He's not like other kids. He's more gentle and sensitive."

"I already told you that I caught him swinging from the light fixture," Blade said, keeping his voice as light as he could. "Would a gentle and sensitive kid do that? Sometimes we see what we want to see rather than the reality."

"Blade," she said in a voice that let him know a reproof was coming.

Yet she didn't have time to continue. The door opened and Detective Sykes walked in, closely followed by Archie and Tim. Archie bounded into the room and jumped up onto the bed, throwing his arms around his mother and holding on tight.

"It's nice to see you back, Detective Sykes," Blade said, watching her hang back to allow Josie's family some space. "Are you fully recovered?"

"I'm good, thank you, Mr. Harding," she replied, pointing to a row of small, neat stitches on her eyebrow. "I have just one small wound." She dropped her voice and led Blade into the corner. "We're very concerned about this latest development. I just can't imagine how a bomb was smuggled into the courthouse without inside help. We've requested all of today's security footage from the courthouse in the hope that it'll give us a lead."

"Josie also received some flowers from Cardwell a few moments ago," he said, making sure to whisper. "The message said she would die tomorrow. Detective Pullman knows all about it."

Detective Sykes took a sharp breath. "It might be wise to keep Josie on lockdown for a couple of days. I'll explain to the judge that she can't risk her life by continuing the trial."

"You think she should be replaced by another attorney?"

"I do," the detective replied with solemnity. "This has gone far enough."

Blade glanced at Josie, cuddling Archie on the bed with a smile of joy mingled with apprehension on her face.

"Josie's come this far. I doubt she'll walk away from Norman now," he said. "This battle is one that she'll want to fight all the way to the finish."

* * *

Josie slipped Oscar into her son's backpack and zipped it up. She checked her list and ticked off the items that had already been included in the suitcase, pushing Blade's concerns to the back of her mind. How dare he accuse her of babying her son? At six years old, Archie was barely out of toddlerhood. At least, that was the way she saw it. Blade might be Archie's father, but he had a lot to learn about how complex he was. Just because Archie sometimes liked to swing from the ceiling now and again didn't mean he was a rough-and-tumble kind of boy. He wasn't. Josie knew him from his head to his toes.

She sat on a chair in Archie's room as a sensation of light-headedness engulfed her. She had discharged herself from the hospital against the doctor's wishes, but there was no way she would allow herself to be kept there overnight while her son prepared to take a road trip.

"You okay, Josie?" Blade asked, walking into the room with Archie in his arms.

Since their son had learned of his unexpected visit to his great-grandparents' house in Dodge City, he had attached himself to his father like a limpet, and it hurt Josie to see the strength of his affections. Archie had barely spoken to her while she packed his suitcase.

"I'm fine," Josie replied, smiling brightly. "How about you, champ?" she said to Archie. "You excited about your trip?"

"I want Dad to come," Archie whined. "I don't want to go without him."

Blade tried to place him on the floor, but Archie refused to let go of his father's neck and clung on for dear life. Blade gave up and allowed his small body to remain curled against his torso. Josie physically ached, watching her son cuddle his father while her own arms remained empty.

"We already talked about this, buddy," Blade said gently. "I need to stay in Wichita and take care of your mom."

Archie was unconvinced by this argument. "But Mom can come, too."

"Mom has to work," Blade said. "She's a very important lawyer—you know that—and lots of people rely on her to help them."

"It's not fair," Archie said, his whiny voice rising.

"Listen to me, son," Blade said, pulling Archie's fingers, one by one, from around his neck and forcing him to stand on his own two feet. "If you and Granddad aren't here to take care of your mom, who's gonna do it, huh?"

Archie thought about this for a few seconds, his face screwed up tight. "I don't know."

"Exactly," Blade said, dropping to a bended

knee to be on his son's level. "You normally do a great job of being Mom's special helper and giving her hugs when she needs them, but if you're not here, then she'll be lonely all by herself. You wouldn't want that, would you?"

Archie shook his head, his blond curls bouncing. "No, sir."

"You won't be away for long," Blade said. "Just long enough for Mom to finish her important job and get your house ready to move back into."

At the mention of his home, Archie perked up. "So you'll give Mom lots of hugs when she's sad?" he asked seriously. "Because that's one of my important jobs."

Blade put his arm around Josie's shoulder. She surprised herself by not flinching or shrugging him off. His arm, in the sleeve of a brushed cotton shirt, was warm and weighty, seemingly naturally suited to resting on her nape and shoulder. In fact, she enjoyed the gesture of affection. She always enjoyed Blade's gestures of affection, no matter how resentful she felt about losing her son's loyalties to him.

"I'll give your mom as many hugs as she needs," Blade said.

Archie smiled knowingly. Josie recognized his expression as one of mischief.

"She looks sad now," Archie said with a downcast face. "I think she needs a big hug right away."

Josie shook her head reprovingly. She knew exactly what her son was up to, but Blade played along, turning and drawing her into a tight embrace. She had no choice but to snake her arms around Blade's waist and rest her head on his torso, breathing in his woody scent. In his gentle hold, she allowed the tension in her body to flow away, breathing in rhythm with the rise of his chest. It was the most relaxed she had felt in many months, and she almost didn't want the moment to end, but Blade finally pulled away with a smile.

"You see?" he said to Archie. "I'm almost as good as you are at hugging Mom."

"Only almost," Archie said, turning to run from the room. "I'll go tell Granddad I'm ready to go."

Josie rolled her eyes. The child's ability to change his mind in a heartbeat was remarkable. She watched him run to the stairs and hook his leg over the banister, preparing to slide all the way to the bottom.

She stepped forward. "No, you're not allowed to do that. Walk down the stairs, please."

But her son, for the first time in his life, openly disobeyed her. He shot her a defiant stare and climbed onto the banister before gliding out of sight on his downward path.

"Archie Bishop!" she called, chasing after him. "You're in so much trouble."

A sudden yelp and stomach-turning crunch stopped her in her tracks. Something had cracked hard onto the wooden floorboards at the bottom of the stairs.

She screamed at the top of her voice, "Archie!"

TEN

Josie didn't know how she got from the top of the stairs to the bottom in barely the blink of an eye, but all she cared about was reaching her boy. When she saw him, she let out a gasp of anguish, seeing him lying limp in her father's arms. She immediately feared the worst.

"He seems okay," Tim said as he lifted Archie into her arms. "Thankfully he fell only about five feet and the table broke his fall, but he's had a nasty shock."

She looked down at her son's face and body, searching every inch of him for signs of injury. She saw none, but she knew he could have unseen injuries. She then focused on his eyes. They were open, blinking as fast as his breathing.

"Sorry, Mom," Archie murmured. "Don't be mad."

She was too focused on checking him over to answer. His pupils seemed dilated, and his expression was a little distant. She turned to Blade, who was standing by her side. Detectives Pullman and Sykes were also in the hallway, drawn by the commotion.

"We need to get him to the hospital," she said. "Right away."

Blade took a few seconds to examine Archie, who smiled at his father in a sheepish way. "Let's not be hasty," he said. "I think he's fine."

"Of course you think he's fine," she snapped. "You and I have completely different ideas about safeguarding Archie's health. I'm sure his leg would need to be hanging off before you agreed to take him to the ER."

"Archie," Blade said, not even bothering to acknowledge her comment. "How do you feel?"

"I'm okay," he said, wriggling out of his mother's arms and standing on his feet. "But I broke the plant." He looked at the floor. "Sorry."

Josie looked sharply at the spot where Archie was pointing. There, on the wooden boards, was a broken china pot, its dark earth spilling out and the leafy plant uprooted. That must've been the crack she had heard. She put her hand to her face, relieved, but she still couldn't let go of the fear that an injury had occurred.

"It doesn't matter about the plant," she said, lifting his chin to force his eyes to meet hers. "Does anything hurt?"

He shook his head.

"It's important that you tell me if you have any pain," she said. It was common for Archie to hide any discomfort if he thought it would upset her. "I'm not mad at you."

Again, Archie shook his head. He was now retreating into his shell, embarrassed at having caused a drama. She wouldn't be able to get him to open up for a good while now. And in the meantime, he could have swelling or bleeding on the brain.

She picked him up again, deciding to act rather than deliberate. "I'm taking him to the ER. You can all stay here if you want to, but I'm going."

Blade kept his voice smooth. "Try to calm down. Tim saw Archie fall, and it wasn't too far or too serious. I think you're overreacting."

This hit a nerve. "What did you say? My son falls from a banister onto a hard wooden floor and you accuse me of overreacting because I want him checked over by a doctor?"

"I have an idea," Detective Sykes said, stepping forward, clearly trying to defuse the tension. "The police have a pathologist on call for forensics at crime scenes. He's a fully qualified doctor, and I'm sure he'd be happy to check Archie over to put your mind at rest. If he's free right now, he could be here in less than ten minutes. Shall I call him?"

"Yes, please do that," Josie said.

She felt Archie's hand grip the hem of her sweater. "Mom, you said you weren't mad, but you are. I'm sorry about the plant. I'll pay for it with my allowance."

This caused her cheeks to flush hot with sadness and shame. "I'm not mad, honey. Really, I'm not." She stroked his head. "I'm just worried about you."

Tears fell down her face, and Archie started to cry, too. He reached up to his father, and Blade deftly lifted him into his arms.

"Hey, buddy," Blade said softly. "Your mom's had a really tough day and she's sad, but she'll be fine."

Blade's words reminded Josie of the blinding flash of the explosion and the heat that followed. The memory did nothing to help stop the tears, but she tried her very best to keep her voice stable.

"Your dad's right, Archie. I'm sad that I won't see you for a while, and I want to make sure you're okay before you leave."

Archie's tears abated a little, and Blade passed him into Tim's arms. "You go with Granddad into the living room and wait for the doctor while I talk to Mom."

"Am I still going to Dodge City?" he asked as he was carried across the hallway by Tim.

Josie wished she could be as bright and cheerful as Blade, who was soothing Archie's fears much better than she was.

"You sure are," he said with a smile. "Detective Pullman is driving you there in the movie car a little later."

Archie punched his fist in the air. This was the name he had given to the black SUVs driven by the detectives, because of the television screens built into the seatbacks.

"Yes!" he said. "I can watch cartoons."

Blade took Josie's hand. "You're cold," he said. "Let's go make some coffee or something."

This sounded like a good idea. She needed something hot and sweet to calm her nerves. Would the anxiety of these last few days ever end? She hated not knowing where Cardwell was, what he was planning or if he would ever be caught. How long would she have to spend apart from her precious son? Would Archie even be well enough to travel to Dodge City, away from the danger?

And was the prediction on the note about to come true? *Tomorrow you die for real.*

Blade placed a mug of coffee in front of Josie, listening to the pathologist talking animatedly to Archie in the living room. Much to Josie's disappointment, their son had requested that only his granddad be present in the room while he was examined, but both Blade and Josie had instantly guessed his reasoning. He didn't want them to start arguing again. That fall from the banister had triggered a highly emotional reaction from his mom, and Archie knew he was responsible. Both parents would need to sit down and have a conversation before he left for Dodge City. Blade wanted Archie to take responsibility for disobeying his mother, yet his son shouldn't harbor too much guilt about the aftermath. The only thing broken was a china pot.

"I'm sorry," Josie said, her face pale. "You were right about Archie. He's not hurt, but I panicked. I'm sure the pathologist will think I'm a hysterical mother."

"Who cares what the pathologist thinks?" Blade said, sitting next to her.

He watched her moisten her full lips and bow her head over her mug, warming her hands around the edges. The fight seemed to have left her body.

"Don't give up, Josie," he said. "I know today was rough, but tomorrow will be better."

She raised her head and looked at him, sending butterflies swirling in his belly.

"How will tomorrow be better?" she asked. "You saw what the note on the flowers said."

"Forget about the note. You're safe."

"I have to accept that Cardwell might succeed," she said in a monotone voice. "I've given it a lot of thought, and I want you to promise me that you'll take good care of our son if the worst happens."

Blade's eyes suddenly filled up. He didn't want to think about this. He didn't want to imagine a life without Josie in it.

"I want you to promise me that you'll take Archie's safety seriously," she continued. "Always make sure he wears a life vest on the water, don't let him climb too high and please listen to his concerns, whatever they are."

"Josie," Blade said, taking her hand, which was still cool despite the warmth of the mug. "You're worrying about nothing. Please stop saying these things."

But she didn't seem to be listening to him. "I worry that you'll try to force Archie to be like you. He might not be comfortable hiking in the woods or learning to shoot guns." She looked at him earnestly. "So don't force him, okay?"

"Archie has his own unique character, and I'll never try to force him to be like anybody else. He is who he is, and I'll love him for the rest of my days." Blade had to stop in order to swallow away the emotion and steady his voice. "I adore our son, Josie, and I'll never let him down."

"It's strange, you know," she said sadly. "I feel

like I've lost him to you already. You're the one he wants all the time."

This recurring theme needed to be put to bed once and for all. "You have to stop thinking like this, Josie. Children need a mother *and* a father equally. Archie will go through phases when he'll switch his attentions between the two of us, depending on what's going on in his life. Right now, he's learning how to assert his independence. He wants to push his boundaries and do things that scare him, like swing from the light fixtures and slide down banisters. It's totally normal, and that's why dads are an essential part of growing up. I'm strong enough to lift and carry him when he needs it, but *only* if he needs it." Blade leaned back in his chair. "If he can do something by himself then I'll let him. I have every faith in him because he's smart and sensible." He smiled. "The smart and sensible part is all because of you, by the way."

He was pleased to see Josie laugh. "I agree."

"Have you ever heard the phrase 'Give me a child until he is seven and I'll show you the man'?" he asked.

She shook her head, obviously wondering why he was going off track.

"It's a phrase that's used in lots of different churches to promote good moral teaching among very small children. Plenty of people think that the character of a child is pretty much all determined by the time he's seven years of age, so early guidance is vital. That means Archie's personality is already almost fully formed, and I have to say that you've done an exceptional job." He swallowed away more emotion. "It's very humbling to know that the woman I love bore my child, sacrificed so much for his happiness and is now letting me back into his life, even though I abandoned you to focus on my selfish needs."

She looked at him in confusion. "You said I was the woman you love. You mean I'm the woman you *loved*, right?"

When he didn't answer right away, her mouth dropped open. "What exactly are you saying, Blade?"

"I'm not sure," he replied. "I think we make a good team. Archie clearly loves having us both under the same roof together. I enjoy being here with you." He dropped his voice. "I more than enjoy it. Even when we disagree, I see a woman of strength and power who makes me proud." He dared to look her in the eye. "I'd like to try again. I'd like to fulfill the promise that I made to you seven years ago."

Josie's eyes widened, and she stood up as if in panic. "You don't have to do this, Blade."

He hadn't expected this reaction, but he wasn't sure what reaction would be normal.

"I'm not saying this because I feel a sense of obligation to you," he said. "You're the mother of my child, but you're more than that to me. I love everything about you." He stopped just short of saying *I love you*. It didn't look like Josie was ready to hear those words yet. "I love being with you."

"This is too sudden, Blade," she said, seemingly breathless. "I don't know what to say."

"You don't have to say anything. Just think about it. Try to stop seeing me as the man who's stealing your son away and try to think of me as the man who's here to back you up. I will always back you up, Josie, always."

She looked a little shell-shocked and simply stared at him. The excruciating silence continued until Archie burst into the room with a beaming smile on his face. He jumped onto a chair to be at ideal hugging height for his mother. Then he curled his arms around her neck.

"The doctor says I have strong bones like a superhero," he said. "So you don't need to be sad anymore, Mom."

"That's great, honey," she said, lifting him into the air. "You're my very own mini superhero."

"And I'm the full-size version," Blade said.

She didn't seem to appreciate his poor attempt at humor. Instead she put Archie onto his feet, ran her hands awkwardly through her hair and took a deep breath before saying, "I'll go check the suitcases one last time. Archie, you play with Dad for a few minutes."

Then she was gone, her mind probably awash with thoughts. After all, he had given her a lot to consider.

Security in the courthouse was the highest Josie had ever seen. Police officers were everywhere, seeming to outnumber the many people packed into the gallery for what she hoped would be the very last day in this high-profile and contentious trial. The protesters who had previously lined the path into the building were nowhere to be seen today. Josie didn't know whether the decision to abandon the protest was voluntary or if the police had forced them to disperse, unwilling to risk a repeat of the explosion yesterday. The trial had yet again been forced to change rooms due to the damage inflicted on their previous location.

Detective Sykes had tried to persuade Josie to put herself on lockdown for the rest of the week, but Josie wouldn't contemplate it. She had made it clear to the judge yesterday that she was ready to immediately continue the trial. He had commandeered another court and announced his decision to reconvene without further delay.

Josie had already been in the building for three hours, only a fraction of which had been spent in the courtroom setting out her case for a dismissal of the charges against her client. She thought her argument was strong, but the decision to grant her motion belonged to the judge. After putting the court in recess, he had gone away to deliberate, leaving Josie and Norman on tenterhooks.

The judge now reentered the room, and she rose from her chair, listening to the murmurings from the public gallery. The atmosphere was electric, and her client was clearly feeling the strain as he reached for her hand to squeeze in a rare show of weakness. Norman was no longer wearing his big overcoat and instead was content to attend court in a regular suit. It was a huge milestone for him, one which mattered to Josie almost as much as the result of the trial itself. Norman had taken the first step in throwing off the shackles that had bound him for his whole adult life. It was inspirational to see.

Josie cast a glance to her right, taking a look at the prosecutor. Allan Sanders hadn't been his usual effervescent self that morning. He hadn't even acknowledged her as she'd walked past him in the corridor, his arrogance and confidence replaced with somberness. His body language was already showing defeat.

"Before I reconvene today's proceedings," the judge began, "may I ask all those present to respect the order of my court. I understand that tensions are running high, but any disruption from the gallery will be dealt with swiftly and decisively." He paused for a breath. The judge had not directly referred to yesterday's explosion but had commended the staff for dealing with what he referred to as a "dark day" in the court's history. "Miss Bishop, Mr. Sanders," he said, looking between the opposing counsels. "Are you ready?"

When both she and Sanders acknowledged the affirmative, the judge picked up a piece of paper in front of him and looked around the courtroom reverently. A hush fell. Josie tried her very hardest to keep her concentration on the judge and his imminent words rather than on the death threat hanging over her. As soon as she had awoken that morning, she had thought of Orlando Cardwell's promise for her that day. However, she knew that Blade was behind her, watching her back, protecting her, praying for her. She was comforted by, and thankful for, his presence, but her exact feelings for him were muddled and confused. Did she love him or was she simply reliant on his strong support? Could she have a future with him or was it wishful thinking on his part? She just didn't know. And at that moment, she couldn't allow Blade's face to settle on her mind. The next few minutes could change Norman's life.

"I have given full consideration to the defense counsel's motion to dismiss the charges against Norman Francis," the judge said. "The prosecution's case hinges quite substantially on the witness testimony of Miss Janice Weeks, the neighbor of the defendant. It is her testimony, and hers alone, that gives credibility to the argument that Mr. Francis deliberately and knowingly led the child inside his home." Murmurings caught in the gallery as people began to guess what the judge's decision might be. He raised his voice slightly. "Yesterday we heard Miss Weeks admit to this court that her testimony is a falsehood, motivated by the bitter feud that exists between her and the defendant. As a result, it has now become apparent that the case for the prosecution has been largely based on a lie."

The murmurings became louder and the judge called for order once again. Josie's heart was hammering. When the words finally came, they were like sweet music to her ears.

"I hereby grant the defense counsel's motion to dismiss all charges against the defendant."

An eruption of joy burst through Josie's chest,

and she craned her neck around to find Blade's face. She didn't need to search hard. He was there, at the back, his wide smile instantly noticeable. Norman hung his head, wiping his thumbs beneath his eyes, and Josie was so very glad to have achieved this result for him.

She barely heard the rest of the judge's words, as he thanked the jurors for their service and told Norman that he was free to depart the court without a stain on his character. All Josie saw was Blade, and all she could think of was his unfailing support and care of her throughout the trial.

Since he had driven through the night from North Carolina, Archie's life had changed beyond measure. She could never have imagined that Blade's return could have such a profound effect on her, too. The idea of the three of them being a family unit suddenly didn't seem so crazy. Blade's words from the previous day returned to her mind: *Try to stop seeing me as the man who's stealing your son away and try to think of me as the man who's here to back you up.* If she could only learn to accept that Blade's parenting style complemented her own rather than undermined it, she could move forward without fear. But she didn't know if it was possible.

The jury rose from their seats and began filing out of the courtroom, accompanied by security officers. The people of the public gallery were standing, some crying and hugging each other. For Lisa Brown's family, the judge's decision must have come as a hefty blow. After eighteen months of waiting, this result would be hard to take. Many people, including Lisa's parents, had convinced themselves of Norman's guilt. And they would now have to accept humbly that they were wrong.

"I expect you'll be celebrating this evening, Josie. Congratulations on your victory."

Josie turned to see Allan Sanders standing close to her, a smile fixed on his face.

"There are no winners today," she replied. "I'm just glad that the truth prevailed in the end." She forced herself to smile back at him. "After all, isn't that why we're all here?"

Sanders glanced around, seeming to check who was listening. Norman was sitting quietly, head bowed. Josie knew he was praying, probably giving a message of thanks, and she had stepped away from him to give him the space he needed.

"I don't know about you, but I could do with winding down after all that's happened," Sanders said. "How about dinner tonight?"

Josie took a second or two to comprehend exactly what her opposing counsel was suggesting.

Was he asking her out on a date? His change in attitude astounded her.

"I'm sorry, Allan," she replied, thankful to have a legitimate excuse to avoid his invitation. "But that's impossible. I'm on lockdown for the rest of the day."

"I see," he said, as if he knew the rejection was coming. "I had forgotten about your difficult situation." He looked at her with an odd mixture of concern and curiosity. "Where are you staying in order to avoid these dreadful death threats?"

She picked up her heavy file of papers from the desk. "I can't discuss that information with anybody. That's the reason it's called a safe house."

She scanned the courtroom, finding Blade standing by the exit door, arms crossed, watching her every move. She smiled at him.

"And is your former SEAL bodyguard staying with you also?" Sanders asked. "You two seem close." He leaned in. "And I must say that I've noticed a striking similarity between your friend and your little boy." He wrinkled his brow. "I met your son once when I saw you at the park a while back. What's his name? Alfie?"

Josie prickled with annoyance. The prosecutor's intrusion was wearing thin. He seemed to be making conversation simply for the sake of it.

"Archie," she corrected him. "Blade is my

son's father." She saw Norman raise his head, his prayer now finished. "And what's more," Josie continued, surprising even herself, "he's a great father. The best there is."

"Glad to hear it," Sanders said, sounding anything but glad. He picked up her briefcase from the floor. "Don't forget this. Can I carry it to your car for you?"

"No, thank you, Allan," she said, taking the bag from him with her free hand. From the corner of her eye, she could see Blade walking in her direction. "I'll be just fine."

"As you wish," he said stiffly, taking one last glance at Norman before heading for a side door out of the courtroom.

Blade reached her side. "Congratulations on a job well done," he said, bending to kiss her on the cheek.

She felt her color rise. Since they had waved goodbye to their son the previous evening, Blade had not mentioned again the prospect of moving to Sedgwick and trying to rekindle their romance.

"Thanks," she said, spotting a few gray hairs peppered into Blade's sandy curls. Had he always had them, and had she simply failed to notice them? She felt as though she was looking at him in a new and more thorough way. "It's a big relief, I can tell you."

Blade jerked his head at Allan Sanders, who had just stridden through the door out of the courtroom. "And what did our cheerful prosecutor have to say?"

"Nothing of any importance," she replied, handing her briefcase to him so she could help Norman to his feet. She kept herself in check just at the last moment. Her tendency to assist those who she assumed were vulnerable was now under control.

Norman stood unaided and held out his hand for her to shake. "Thank you, Josie," he said. "The Lord provided me with the best defender I could ever have needed, and I'm so grateful for your efforts."

Josie ignored the hand, placed her file on the desk and drew Norman into a hug. His body felt small and awkward, as if he was unused to such shows of affection. But when she pulled back, the smile on his face spoke a thousand words.

"It was a pleasure to help you, Norman," she said. "Like the judge said, you can go home without a stain on your character."

"I'm grateful for more than your efforts in the courtroom, Josie," Norman said. "You exposed my cerebral palsy to everybody when you made me stand and take off my coat yesterday. At the time, I wanted the ground to open up and swallow me, but now I feel liberated. When I et home this afternoon, I'll be burning that big vercoat I've always worn."

"Good for you," Josie said. "I can't tell you ow happy that makes me." She pointed to his g. "But first, let's go get that GPS tracker re- oved from your ankle."

She felt Blade's arm curl around her shoul- er. "And then I think that a very special pub- c defender needs to have a celebratory dinner ooked for her by a master chef." He leaned to hisper into her ear. "And by that, I mean me."

She smiled, yet her stomach jolted as if she ere in an elevator. Blade was trying to be up- eat, but he had just reminded her that she would ow be returning to the safe house, where she ust hide out for the foreseeable future. Now at the trial was over and Archie was safely in odge City, there would be no distractions to ke her mind off the danger. It was just she and lade riding out the storm, hoping and praying at Cardwell would soon be caught.

But at this moment, nobody had a clue where ardwell was. He could even be right there in e courthouse, just waiting, biding his time. nd there was nothing she could do to stop him.

Blade was on edge, but he hoped he was hid- ig it well. He had been worried all day, con- tantly scanning the area around Josie for signs

of Cardwell. If this convict was clever enough t
bring a bomb into a courthouse, then he was de
initely clever enough to find a way to get close t
her. Blade did not intend to let that happen, an
he stood guard while Josie walked quickly fror
the back door of the courthouse into the waitin
car in the lot. Both he and Detective Sykes wer
on high alert, ensuring that the path betwee
Josie and the car was totally clear.

The dismissal of the charges had given Blad
a well-needed boost to his morale, but it fur
damentally changed nothing. Josie was still i
danger, and he had no idea when her situatio
would improve. Only Cardwell's arrest woul
give him the conclusion he needed.

He watched her slide into the backseat of th
SUV, swinging her long legs into the footwel
Today she was wearing a tailored black pantsui
and he wondered if the funereal attire was influ
enced by the death threat hanging over her head

"All clear," he said, sliding into the seat nex
to her and buckling up. "Let's go make that cel
ebratory dinner I was talking about."

She smiled weakly. His attempts to cheer he
up had largely fallen flat, but he had to try. He
happiness meant more to him than his own, an
he couldn't bear to see her so despondent.

Josie checked her watch. "There are still te

hours of this day left," she said. "That's ten more hours for Cardwell to fulfill his promise."

"Your location is a secret to all but a tiny handful of people," Blade said. "There's no way Cardwell will find you."

The emotion of the day seemed to come spilling out. "I just want my life to be back to normal," she said, suppressing a sob. "I want my son back." She placed a hand over her heart. "I've never been away from him before. I hate the thought of going home to an empty house."

"It won't be empty," Blade said. "I'm there, and I'm committed to staying with you for as long as it takes."

She dried her eyes with a tissue. "That's kind of you, Blade," she said. "But you have an important training regimen to stick to, and the Invictus Games are in a few months. You can't miss the most important sporting event of your whole life."

He hadn't known the true strength of his feelings for her until that moment. "Yes, I can."

She looked at him in shock. "Are you serious? You'd miss the Invictus Games for me?"

He didn't even hesitate in his reply. "Of course I would."

She opened her mouth and closed it again, like a fish out of water.

Blade decided that it was now or never. He had to make plain his emotions.

"I love you, Josie," he said. "If your life is in danger, I'd miss every single Invictus Games for the rest of my life. You mean more to me than any number of medals."

He heard her gasp, obviously surprised by his admission. Yet it was simple to him. He loved her, and his loyalty to her surpassed any sporting event, no matter how important.

"I'm honored," she said quietly. "But I can't ask that much of you."

"You're not asking me to do it," he said. "I'm offering it freely."

"This is all too much, Blade," Josie said. "I need some time to think about it."

He turned his head to look at the cars behind. "Take as much time as you need. I'm not going anywhere."

She fell mute again. Blade noticed Detective Sykes's expression in the rearview mirror change, and his focus shifted to what was going on outside the car. Detective Sykes suddenly pressed hard on the gas pedal, sending the car surging forward. She safely ran through a red light, and the car behind did exactly the same. Somebody was on their tail.

Blade reached for his weapon. It was time to prove that he was as good as his word.

ELEVEN

Josie pressed her hands together. She didn't want to even glance behind at the car pursuing them. She knew who would be sitting in the driver's seat. There was no point in looking into Cardwell's eyes as he chased her down.

"Please, Lord," she said under her breath. "Let this be the last time."

"How did he find us?" Detective Sykes said anxiously, swerving the car through traffic. "I know he didn't follow us from the courthouse. I'm sure of it."

"How he found us is irrelevant right now," Blade said. "What's more important is shaking him off." He pulled his gun. "Or stopping him in his tracks."

"No, Blade," Josie said, watching the detective take them into a congested area. "It's too dangerous to shoot here. There are too many people around."

He nodded. "I know. It's just a precaution."

"There's a police station a couple of miles away," the detective said. "I'll head there. We can get there quicker than backup will take to arrive."

Maybe Cardwell sensed their plan, or maybe his frustration at failing to kill Josie finally bubbled to the boiling point. He sped up his vehicle and rammed them hard. Josie flew forward, her seat belt preventing her from connecting with the front seats. This time, she did look behind, and Cardwell had done significantly more damage to his own car than to theirs. His hood was crumpled, steam was leaking from the engine and the windshield was cracked in his sleek black sports car, which, like everything he'd ever had in life, she assumed was stolen.

She barely had time to compose herself when he rammed them again, and this time Detective Sykes veered across the street, struggling to retain control of their SUV. Josie heard the tires squealing on the asphalt and assumed a crash position, preparing herself for a collision. But no impact came. Instead she felt Blade's body brush hers as he made a swift movement. When she lifted her head, she saw him in the front passenger seat, helping Detective Sykes to steady the vehicle. With one hand he held the wheel and in the other he held his gun.

"The police department is right up ahead,"

Detective Sykes said. "Let's see if Cardwell hangs around once we pull into the lot."

But Cardwell obviously knew what was awaiting him and didn't intend to fall into a trap, because when Josie looked around, he was gone. The road behind stretched long and empty, and she didn't know whether to feel relieved or saddened that he had vanished. She was safe for now, but it would simply delay the inevitable.

"Shouldn't we stop at the police station?" she asked, watching the building sail right by.

"There's no point," Detective Sykes said, looking at her through the rearview mirror. "Now that Cardwell has gone, there's not a lot they can do. Let's get you back to the safe house as soon as we can."

With that, she picked up her radio and began to relay the information regarding Cardwell's location and vehicle to all patrols.

"Detective Sykes is right," Blade said, turning around. "We should get you out of here immediately."

She held her hand out, a sudden sensation of dread causing a chill to sweep over her skin. "I'm scared, Blade. I have a really bad feeling."

He took her hand and held it tight. "He's gone. Don't worry."

But somehow, Josie knew that Cardwell hadn't

gone far. He was close by. And he would reveal himself again later. She was sure of it.

Blade was glad to see the safe house come into view. The return journey to their hideaway had given him grave concerns. Just exactly how had Cardwell ended up on their tail on the highway? Was the escaped convict fortunate enough to have stumbled across them, or was he tipped off by somebody? Blade was absolutely sure that nobody followed them from the courthouse, so Cardwell must have jumped onto their tail at least ten miles into the journey. The last thing Josie needed right now was a mole in the police operation.

Josie once again reached for his hand as they walked into the house and squeezed his fingers tight. He had noticed that she was becoming more tactile with him since Archie had left for Dodge City, often brushing his arm or holding his hand. He wasn't sure if she was simply missing her son or if she was letting him know she was ready to restart their romance. But he guessed that this wasn't the time to ask.

Detective Pullman was on the telephone when they entered the living room, sitting hunched over his notepad, writing quickly as he occasionally muttered, "uh-uh" and "I see." The news he was receiving was obviously serious, and as soon as he hung up the phone, Josie must have feared the worst.

"Is Archie okay?" she asked, dropping her briefcase and sitting on the couch. "Did something happen?"

"Archie is fine," Detective Pullman said reassuringly. "That call was from one of the US marshals looking for Cardwell."

Blade felt a surge of hope. "Did they pick him up?"

"Sadly not," the detective replied. "The police patrols are still looking for the stolen car he was driving."

Blade sat next to Josie. "So what was the call about?"

"The marshals have been interviewing members of staff at the courthouse today in order to find out who helped Cardwell smuggle the explosive device into the building. One of the security officers admitted that he allowed an unchecked bag to come in through the back door yesterday. He said that the person carrying the bag told him it contained personal items, and because he was a well-respected attorney, the guard agreed to turn a blind eye."

One person instantly came to Blade's mind. "Are you talking about Allan Sanders?"

"Yes," the detective replied. "It could be a simple coincidence. We have no proof that Mr.

Sanders's bag contained any explosives, but the marshals are trying to track him down for questioning."

"Trying to track him down?" Blade repeated. "You mean he's gone missing?"

"He's not at his office or at home, and nobody seems to know where he is."

Josie, who had been listening closely, now spoke. "Allan asked me out for dinner this evening. He said he needed to wind down."

Blade found an unpleasant feeling settling in his stomach, something akin to jealousy. "You didn't mention this earlier."

Josie shrugged. "I didn't think it was important. He didn't seem to want me to accept his offer. I think he was just making conversation. I told him I was on lockdown, and then he asked where I was staying…"

"Whoa, hold up a minute," Blade interrupted. "He asked you where the safe house was?"

"Yes." She wrinkled her brow. "I didn't really think anything of it at the time. I assumed he was just being curious."

Blade thought of how Cardwell had found them so easily on the road. Could he have been tipped off about their route? "You didn't tell him, did you?"

"Of course not," she replied. "I'd never tell him anything important."

"That's not all the marshals found out today," Detective Pullman said, turning over a page on his notepad. "The clerk at the bank who leaked details of an account supposedly belonging to Norman Francis has now admitted to lying. She forged bank statements showing cash amounts of ninety thousand dollars deposited in Norman's name, which she subsequently passed on to the media for publication."

Blade was incredulous. "Why would anybody do that?"

"She was bribed with a lot of money?" the detective replied. "She says it was all arranged online, and the cash was wired straight into her bank account. She doesn't know who was behind it or why."

"I think it's pretty obvious why," Josie said. "The lie was created in order to whip up a protest about Norman using a public defender. Somebody wanted to make sure that I'd be forced to run through a mob of angry demonstrators every day. Somebody wanted to see me suffer. Cardwell is bound to be behind it."

This theory didn't add up in Blade's mind. "But Cardwell is a convicted criminal. Where would he get a large amount of money to bribe a bank clerk? He must have had financial help from somebody."

"Or maybe it wasn't Cardwell who bribed the

clerk," Detective Sykes suggested, walking from the doorway where she had been standing. "And maybe it wasn't Cardwell who sent the flowers to the hospital, either."

Josie swiveled around. "What are you thinking?"

"Well, we now know that Allan Sanders smuggled an unchecked bag into the courthouse yesterday," she replied. "He doesn't seem to like you much, and he was desperate to win this case. It's not so crazy to suspect that he might've been helping Cardwell to terrorize you, hoping to destroy your confidence in order to sabotage the trial."

Josie didn't seem convinced. "Allan's a ruthless character, and he certainly doesn't like me, but he wouldn't go that far." She looked at Blade. "Would he?"

"There's only one person who can answer that question," said Blade, "and that's Sanders himself." Josie was shaking slightly, and he knew that she was genuinely terrified by these latest revelations. "I'm sure the marshals will pick him up soon."

The room was suddenly filled with ringtones, as both of the detectives' cell phones began to ring. They exchanged worried glances, checked the displays and answered in unison.

"It looks like our suspicions about Sanders

were correct," Detective Sykes said after a few seconds of listening. "He's on the run. There's a police pursuit on the outskirts of Wichita, and he's apparently showing no intention of stopping." She pointed to the other room and gestured to Detective Pullman. "We'll take these calls in the kitchen."

When they had gone, Josie put her head in her hands. "I don't believe that Allan could be Cardwell's accomplice. He's meant to be an upholder of the law."

"That's obviously not the way Sanders sees it," Blade said. "But at least he's close to being captured. And once he's in custody, I figure that Cardwell won't be far behind."

"Do you think so?"

He touched her cheek. "I do, so don't look so worried."

Josie's face lifted as if she was truly allowing herself to believe Blade's words. "Could this really be over soon? Could we really start looking to the future instead of living just for today?"

"I hope so," he replied, conscious of how close Josie's face had gotten to his. Her wide eyes were staring at him. "What kind of future do you see?" he asked.

Her lips drew even nearer to his. "I'm not sure, but you're right about one thing. Archie needs you to be a constant in his life. No matter how good a mom I think I am, I can never replace a father's love. I'm sorry for shutting you out." She blinked quickly. "I've been a fool for failing to see what an honorable man you are."

"Does this mean what I think it means?" he asked, feeling her soft lips brush his.

He didn't get his answer. The moment was destroyed by the door bursting open and Detective Sykes rushing in.

"Sanders is heading straight for the safe house," she said. "We don't know how he's found us, but it looks like he's coming for you."

Josie felt as though someone had landed a blow to her gut and knocked the breath out of her.

"How far away is he?" Blade asked, pulling out his gun.

"Around five minutes," Detective Sykes said, her voice high with urgency. "We have to go right now. Don't take anything. Just go as you are."

Josie's mind raced. Sanders had betrayed his public office, and now he was coming to finish the job that Cardwell had failed to do.

She felt Blade grab her hand and lead her from the room. "Let's go."

"My briefcase," she said, stooping to pick it up.

The leather bag contained all her most important paperwork for the trial, not to mention her cell phone on which Archie would call. It was the only thing she needed to take with her.

"I'll take it," Blade said, grabbing it from her hand and slinging it over his shoulder. "But don't take anything else. We have no time."

He turned to her and smiled, defusing the tension. Her heart leaped with gratitude for his presence there. He had been her rock throughout her ordeal.

Detective Sykes was already in the SUV, engine running. Detective Pullman ushered them inside the vehicle before taking his own seat in the passenger side. Josie heard the faint sounds of sirens in the distance. Was this the sound of Sanders speeding her way? Detective Sykes clearly thought so, as she floored the gas pedal and sped out of the driveway, tires squealing on the asphalt. Josie leaned heavily onto her right side, falling into Blade's firm torso. He sat bolt upright, gun in hand, constantly checking behind them.

As the sirens grew fainter, a new sound reached Josie's ears. It was the ring of her cell phone, and she pulled her briefcase onto the seat to rummage around inside.

"Leave it," Blade said.

Josie wasn't prepared to do that. "It could be Archie. I don't want him to worry."

But it wasn't Archie. When she looked at the display, the name she read sent a jolt of shock through her. It said A. SANDERS.

She and Blade stared between each other and the cell for a few seconds before Josie pressed the answer button and activated the speakerphone so that all occupants of the vehicle would be able to hear.

"Allan," she said. "What do you want?"

His reply was rushed, harassed and slightly slurred, as if he had been drinking. "Josie, I'm so sorry. I was on my way to apologize to you when the police started following me, and I panicked and ran. They blocked off your street and herded me onto the interstate, but I'll be facing a spike strip soon." She heard the sirens on his tail. "I can't let myself be arrested without making things right with you."

"What do you need to apologize for, Allan?" she asked, keeping her tone neutral. "What did you do?"

"I set you up," he said, a sob breaking his voice. "I'm the one who's been harassing you with letters and phone calls. I even threw a brick through your window."

"What? You did that to me?"

"I just wanted you to walk away from the

case," he replied. "I know how tough you are to beat. I thought the public defender's office would assign a different attorney once the threats started. I never intended to hurt you, but you just wouldn't quit."

The pieces began to fall into place. "Were you behind the organized protests?"

"Yes. I paid an employee at the bank to tell the newspapers that Norman had thousands of dollars hidden away. Then I stirred things up on social media and got people to come out and demonstrate. I really needed to win this case. I'm only one more failed trial away from losing my job as state prosecutor." He broke off for a moment. "You know how badly I've been doing, Josie. I've totally lost my touch. And I think I lost my mind along with it."

Josie could barely believe what she was hearing. "What about the bomb? Did you bring that inside the courtroom?"

"I promise I didn't know what was inside," he said. "One of the protesters told me he wanted to set off harmless smoke bombs to create maximum disruption in the public gallery. I took him at his word, and I smuggled the bag inside. I had no idea it contained an explosive. I left the bag where he told me to leave it, and he must've detonated it remotely." Sanders's words became more slurred, and she suspected he was drinking even while driving. "I never wanted you to get hurt. I just wanted to scare you. That's all I wanted to do."

Now her anger was rising. "Someone died yesterday because of you."

"I'm so sorry."

Josie wondered whether he heard how pathetic his apology was. Allan Sanders had started the campaign of terror against her, and Cardwell had successfully hidden behind it.

"What about the flowers in the hospital?" she asked. "I guess you sent those, too?"

"Flowers?" he repeated, clearly confused. "What flowers?"

Then she knew the promise to end her life was real. It had definitely come from Cardwell.

"I'm ashamed of you," she said, raising her voice. "You're a disgrace to the law profession."

"I know that," he said despondently. "I even knew Janice Weeks was lying right from the start. When you've been a prosecutor as long as I have, you learn to recognize the signs. But I didn't care. I put her on the witness stand anyway. And when you exposed her, I was jealous of your skill and wanted vengeance, so I did something I'll regret for the rest of my life."

A deathly chill slid across her skin. "What did you do, Allan?"

"I put…" He stopped abruptly. She heard a

loud bang through the speaker. The sound must have been created by the spike strip Sanders had talked about.

"Ask him how he found you," Blade said anxiously in the silence. "He said he was on his way to the safe house."

"Allan," she said, realizing that he was only seconds away from arrest. She had to use them wisely. "How did you find me?"

She heard the police shouting orders at Sanders to exit the vehicle.

"Allan," she repeated, louder this time. "How did you find me?"

"I put a GPS tracker in your briefcase," he said. A sound of smashing glass could be heard in the background. "Somebody asked me to do it."

"Who?"

"The same guy who gave me the bag to take into the courtroom. The guy who seems to want you dead."

Then he was gone. Josie grabbed her briefcase, opened it up and tipped the contents over her lap. Her papers fell out in a cascade, along with pens, scribbled notes and packs of gum. The last thing to fall was a small, round device, sleek and black with an illuminated red light on the top. Her mouth fell open and she held it in her palm, frozen.

Blade snatched it from her hand, opened the window and threw it out. But he was too late. She knew this even before she saw Cardwell standing in the deserted road with an explosives vest covering his torso.

"No!" Detective Sykes shouted as she slammed on the brakes to avoid plowing into the man blocking their path.

Josie looked out the window, trying to decipher their location. They seemed to be in an industrial district, full of warehouses and factories, and it was eerily quiet.

"There's a union strike happening this week," Detective Sykes said as she put the car in Reverse. "There's nobody here. I'm getting us out of here."

As the car lurched backward, a loud explosion rocked the street, and a stone wall fell onto the road behind them. A pile of bricks scattered along the ground, sending a dust cloud swirling up into the air. They were trapped.

Detective Pullman yanked the radio out of its cradle. "Emergency, all units, immediate assistance required."

Josie watched Cardwell walk slowly and deliberately toward the vehicle, his hand holding a device that she assumed was the detonator for his explosives vest. In the other hand he held a gun, which he now raised out front, seeking out her face and taking aim.

"Blade," she said, turning to reach for him.

But Blade was gone, his door left wide open. She gasped and put a hand over her mouth in abject shock. Nothing had prepared her for the possibility that he would abandon her when she needed him most.

"Why?" she said out loud. "Why did you leave me?"

She didn't know if she would ever get the opportunity to ask him this question in person, because Cardwell barked an order that she could not disobey.

"Either you do what I say or everybody dies right here, right now."

Blade settled himself beneath the vehicle, watching Cardwell walk steadily toward his intended target. The detonator he was carrying could have been a fake, as could the explosives vest, but he couldn't take any chances on that. Josie's life was hanging in the balance.

"I'm wearing enough Semtex to blow us all into Oklahoma," Cardwell yelled. "So why don't you all get out of the car nice and slow." He held up the detonator with his thumb firmly pressed on top. "And if any of you are thinking of shooting me, then you'll be signing your own death warrant, because this thing is set to explode two seconds after my thumb leaves the button."

Blade heard the car doors open, and three sets of hesitant feet planted themselves on the ground. He saw Josie's high-heeled shoes move slowly toward the front of the car. Was she wondering where he was? Was she assuming he had left her without as much as a backward glance?

"It's not fair to involve these detectives," she said, her voice shaking. "Let them leave, and I'll go with you without causing any trouble."

Cardwell laughed horribly. "That sounds like the best idea you've ever had, Miss Bishop." His tone became hard and bitter. "Why didn't you have great ideas like that when you were representing me in court, huh?"

Blade shifted a little forward. He needed Cardwell to move a couple of feet in his direction. If this crazed convict was telling the truth, there were only two seconds between Josie and certain death. If Blade was going to tackle Cardwell, Cardwell had to come closer.

"We're not leaving you, Josie," Detective Sykes said.

Blade sensed that both detectives were aiming their weapons at Cardwell, yet they would be unable to shoot for fear of setting off an explosion that would instantly kill them all. Similarly, if they tried to flee, Cardwell could pick them off with bullets. He had cleverly thought this through.

"You're welcome to stay," Cardwell said sneeringly. "But I must insist that you bleed."

A gunshot cracked through the air. Josie screamed, and Blade gave an involuntary jump beneath the vehicle. Detective Sykes dropped like a stone to the ground, her eyes locking with Blade's as her head hit the asphalt. She had been shot in the abdomen and was holding the wound with her hand.

"Save her," the detective mouthed to Blade. Then she closed her eyes. Detective Pullman rushed to her side and sank to his knees next to her, trying to stem the bleeding.

"Miss Bishop and I are going on a little road trip," Cardwell said nonchalantly, walking to the prone detective.

The SUV key was lying on the ground where Detective Sykes had dropped it when she fell. Cardwell kicked at the key with his foot. "Pick that up," he ordered Josie. "For once in your life, do something useful."

Josie crouched low and extended her fingers toward the key. That was when she saw Blade, and he saw a smile pass across her lips, almost imperceptible, but definitely a smile.

"Where's your friend?" Cardwell asked as she stood up. "The big guy who's always stuck to you like glue. Did he get bored sick of you or something?"

"Something like that," Josie said.

Cardwell laughed as if he enjoyed this particular thought. He then stepped over Detective Sykes's body, where her colleague was still desperately trying to save her, and opened the car door.

"You'll have to drive," he said. "As you can see, I'm otherwise indisposed."

Josie suddenly gave a huge shout of "Now!" and jumped to the side, giving Blade a perfect opportunity to grip Cardwell's leg and yank it toward him. Cardwell yelled out in surprise as his whole body jerked backward and he toppled over like a felled tree, cracking his head on the ground. His hand bounced from the detonator, and his gun clattered across the asphalt. Blade rolled from beneath the car in a split second, grabbing the detonator in the process and pressing his own thumb on the button. He grimaced, awaiting the explosion, but none came. Thankfully he'd acted quickly enough.

"Run!" he yelled to Josie. Yet she didn't move. She seemed frozen to the spot.

Cardwell was kicking and fighting, trying to pull Blade's thumb from the button. The detonator was attached to the vest with wires, so Blade was unable to remove the device from Cardwell. His only hope was to subdue him.

Then Detective Pullman appeared and restrained Cardwell's arms at his sides as the convicted fraudster gnashed his teeth and growled in frustration.

"I got him pinned down," the detective said. "Backup should be here in a few minutes. Let's keep him steady until then."

"I'll never stop," Cardwell yelled, trying to buck his body beneath the confinement. "I'll escape again, and I'll make you pay."

"Shut up," Blade said, sitting on Cardwell's legs and holding the detonator steady in his right hand. "Nobody cares what you have to say."

"*She* cares," Cardwell said, his eyes flicking to Josie. "She knows what I'm capable of."

"She also knows what *I'm* capable of," Blade said, pulling one of Cardwell's gloves from his hand and stuffing it into the deranged man's mouth.

"That's right," Josie said, finally finding her voice and bending down to look her nemesis in the eye. "So do your worst, because we'll be ready."

Cardwell's muffled cries mingled with the sound of faraway sirens. It sounded like he was saying, "Get off me."

"Oh, I'm not going anywhere," Blade said,

looking up at Josie with a broad smile on his face. "And that's a promise I intend on keeping forever."

Josie sat close to Blade on the sofa in the safe house, her fingers laced through his. She never wanted to let go of him. His courage and quick thinking had saved not only her life but also the lives of the two detectives. Detective Sykes had been rushed to the hospital and given an emergency blood transfusion and was now undergoing surgery to repair damage to her abdominal wall. But she was in good hands, and she would pull through.

Blade lifted his forearm, taking hers with it, and kissed the back of her hand. "I love you, you know that?"

She smiled, feeling something like a somersault take place inside her belly. "And I think I love you, too, Blade."

He raised an eyebrow. "You *think*?"

"You gotta prove yourself first," she said playfully. "I don't give my heart to just anybody."

"Okay," he said, shifting his body to face hers. He eyed the clock. "I figure we have about five minutes before the car arrives to take us back to your house in Sedgwick. Just how can I prove myself in that time?"

She leaned in close and pursed her lips. "I'll give you a clue."

"I'll give it my best shot," he said, pressing his mouth onto hers.

She wound her arms around his neck. His best shot was all she needed.

EPILOGUE

The roar in the stadium was deafening as the crowd cheered the athletes onto the field for the opening ceremony of the Invictus Games. Josie craned her neck to see Blade among the American delegation, some striding out onto the track with prosthetic limbs, others in state-of-the-art wheelchairs.

Although Josie was seated in the front row and on ground level with the athletes, she still felt a hundred miles away from the action. She wished she could be out there with Blade, but this was his moment to shine—the moment he had trained long and hard for.

"I see him, I see him," shouted Archie from his higher vantage point on top of his grand-dad's shoulders. He waved manically. "Hey, Dad! We're over here."

"I don't think he can see us, honey," Josie said, casting her mind back to when seeing Archie wobbling on her father's shoulders would have

nduced an anxiety attack. But not anymore.
he was learning how to relax and let Archie
ake more risks. She even allowed Blade to take
im into the deep end of the swimming pool. It
vasn't much of a risk, but it was a start.

The four members of Blade's former SEAL
.nit were also there with her, waving flags and
anners on which messages of support had been
vritten. Jack, Cole, Dillon and Tyler were ac-
ompanied by their wives and children. Blade's
ld buddies had welcomed her back into the fold
vith plenty of hugs and affection. She felt as
hough she truly belonged.

"I think he's looking for us," Jack said, stand-
ng with his wife, Rebecca. Two blonde teenage
;irls and a younger boy waved beside him, their
ands covered with large foam fingers. Jack
upped his hands over his mouth and yelled,
Blade! Over here."

Dillon threw his head back and laughed.
There's no way he'd be able to hear us. We
eed some kind of signal."

"I have just the thing," Tyler said, grabbing a
ackpack from the floor and opening it up. He
ulled a large flag from the pocket and unfurled
t. It showed the SEAL trident, jet-black against
white background. "Let's hold this at each cor-
er, guys. He's bound to see it."

The men spread out and pulled the flag taut,

holding it above their heads, forcing Archie to scramble off his grandfather's shoulders and si on his own seat. The wind caught the fabric, and it billowed in the wind, sending the insignia ris ing upward. From beneath the canopy, Josie saw Blade walking around the bend of the running track, still in delegation formation, and he wa: looking straight in their direction with a huge grin on his face.

"He definitely sees us now," Cole said, pulling the flag off their heads and folding it. "A SEAL always notices the trident."

Archie began to bounce up and down in his seat. "He's coming over," he squealed, pointing at his father, who had broken away from his teammates to run to them. His prosthesis was on full display below his shorts, and the way his legs moved powerfully across the grass was impressive.

Blade's SEAL buddies all crowded around him, slapping him on the back and talking ani- matedly, but he sidestepped in order to come face-to-face with Josie. She threw her arms around him.

"Go get 'em, Tiger," she said. "I'll be watch- ing every second."

He glanced behind, where the American ath- letes were continuing their lap of honor along-

ide veterans of many others countries across
ne world.

"I'd better get back," he said, cupping her face
nd kissing her lips. "But Archie has something
or you." He winked at his son. "You can give
: to her now."

Archie let out a high-pitched yelp of delight as
e dug deep into his jacket pocket and pulled out
 small white box. He held it up to his mother,
eaming like a cat who'd gotten the cream.

Josie's mouth dropped open and she turned
ack to the field, yelling out, "Is this what I think
t is?"

Blade ran backward as he went to rejoin his
eammates, his sandy curls bouncing just the
ame way as Archie's always did. "Not exactly,"
e said. "But I hope you'll like it."

Josie took the box from Archie's hand and
lipped open the lid. What faced her was not
what she had been expecting. Instead of a glint-
ng diamond, there was a folded piece of paper,
which she opened up to read.

In Blade's distinctive sloping handwriting
vere the words,

I had no time to shop for a ring, but it's on
my list of things to do.

She broke off to laugh. Blade had been busy

selling his auto body shop in North Carolina, a
well as training hard for the games and spend
ing every spare moment with her and Archie i
Sedgwick. She didn't need a ring. It wasn't im
portant. She cast her eyes back to the paper and
continued to read.

> I love you and Archie more than I can ever
> express. Let's be a real family. Let's get
> married. What do you say?

She held the note close to her chest as sh
breathed in this moment. With the roar of th
crowd buzzing in her ears, she filled her lung
with air and screamed out her reply.
"Yes!"

* * * * *

Dear Reader,

Blade and Josie's story is the fifth and final installment of my Navy SEAL Defenders miniseries, and I hope you have enjoyed each and every one. I have genuinely loved getting to know all five heroes of the series, learning to understand their strengths and weaknesses and breathing life into their characters. Blade was perhaps the most complex hero of all, a man who has been forced to adapt to being a disabled man in an able-bodied world. He is my favorite character of the series—a man strong enough to protect Josie, yet tender enough to gently challenge her insensitive attitude.

When Josie and Blade reunite, it is inevitable that tensions flare. Josie has been a parent for six years, but Blade is thrown right in at the deep end and must quickly adjust not only to being a father but also to being a protector for his newly found family. With a little reliance on his faith he rises to the occasion and becomes Josie's surprising rock of support. I very much enjoyed giving these two a happy-ever-after.

The character of Archie is based on a real little boy of the same name, who has beautiful blond curls and a face full of freckles and is perhaps the most wonderfully mischievous boy I have ever known. He was a great help when fleshing out the character of Archie (it was his idea to introduce a budgie named Sherbet into the story), so I'd like to say a big thank-you to him for his fantastic input.

I look forward to welcoming you as a reader again.

Blessings,
Elisabeth

Get 2 Free Books,
Plus 2 Free Gifts—
just for trying the Reader Service!

Love Inspired®

LI17

HOMETOWN HEARTS ♥

YES! Please send me **The Hometown Hearts Collection** in Larger Print. This collection begins with 3 FREE books and 2 FREE gifts in the first shipment. Along with my 3 free books, I'll also get the next 4 books from the Hometown Hearts Collection, in LARGER PRINT, which I may either return and owe nothing, or keep for the low price of $4.99 U.S./ $5.89 CDN each plus $2.99 for shipping and handling per shipment*. If I decide to continue, about once a month for 8 months I will get 6 or 7 more books, but will only need to pay for 4. That means 2 or 3 books in every shipment will be FREE! If I decide to keep the entire collection, I'll have paid for only 32 books because 19 books are FREE! I understand that accepting the 3 free books and gifts places me under no obligation to buy anything. I can always return a shipment and cancel at any time. My free books and gifts are mine to keep no matter what I decide.

262 HCN 3432 462 HCN 3432

Name	(PLEASE PRINT)	
Address		Apt. #
City	State/Prov.	Zip/Postal Code

Signature (if under 18, a parent or guardian must sign)

Mail to the **Reader Service**:

IN U.S.A.: P.O. Box 1867, Buffalo, NY. 14240-1867
IN CANADA: P.O. Box 609, Fort Erie, Ontario L2A 5X3

* Terms and prices subject to change without notice. Prices do not include applicable taxes. Sales tax applicable in NY. Canadian residents will be charged applicable taxes. This offer is limited to one order per household. All orders subject to approval. Credit or debit balances in a customer's account(s) may be offset by any other outstanding balance owed by or to the customer. Please allow 4 to 6 weeks for delivery. Offer available while quantities last. Offer not available to Quebec residents.

Your Privacy—The Reader Service is committed to protecting your privacy. Our Privacy Policy is available online at www.ReaderService.com or upon request from the Reader Service.

We make a portion of our mailing list available to reputable third parties that offer products we believe may interest you. If you prefer that we not exchange your name with third parties, or if you wish to clarify or modify your communication preferences, please visit us at www.ReaderService.com/consumerschoice or write to us at Reader Service Preference Service, P.O. Box 9062, Buffalo, NY. 14240-9062. Include your complete name and address.

HHBPA1